CONCERT
HALL
HIT

CONCERT HALL HIT

A DARCY GAUGHAN MYSTERY

J.C. KENNEY

LEVEL
BEST BOOKS

Author Photo Credit: Amy Pangburn Photography

First edition

ISBN: 978-1-68512-334-5

Cover art by Level Best Designs

This book was professionally typeset on Reedsy.
Find out more at reedsy.com

This is for all the concert goers out there. There's nothing better than live music.

Chapter One

I f she could have gone back in time, Darcy Gaughan would have said no to the man who screwed her over worse than the most vile and despicable Ponzi scheme architect in the history of the planet. Instead, she'd taken the high road and chosen forgiveness. And said "Yes," when Derek Tufnell asked her for a favor.

Now, in the present, there were over a hundred music fans queued up on the sidewalk in front of the store, waiting for their opportunity to meet the very same rock and blues living legend.

She closed her eyes and asked the spirits above to help make sure the next ninety minutes went off without a hitch. And that the recent disturbing rumors regarding Derek weren't true.

"Okay, peeps." Darcy clapped her hands. "Here's the deal. Customers come through the door and go straight down the main aisle to Derek's table. They can get a max of two things signed. Then, they can browse for a while or come straight to me to pay for their purchases."

Charlotte Ryan, Darcy's right-hand woman and general manager of Marysburg Music, raised her hand. "What about the drawing for the tickets for tonight's show?"

"Got that covered." Hank Greenbaum, his gray hair slightly askew, bustled out of the record store's office with a role of carnival tickets in his hand. "Each person gets a ticket when they enter. One half goes in the jar on the table. They keep the other half for the drawing at the end of the event."

"Excellent." Darcy surveyed the scene. Everything seemed to be in place. "Are we missing anything, Derek?"

The guitar hero brushed aside a lock of gray hair from his brow and raised his bottle of flavored sparkling water. It was a high-end brand imported from Wales with a name Darcy had trouble pronouncing.

"Ready to rock and roll. And before we begin, I want to personally thank the dear Ms. Gaughan for putting this little event together. I appreciate it more than words can say."

A thrill ran through Darcy. At an event like this in the past, Derek would have been holding a bottle of scotch instead of water. And propositioning any young woman in sight instead of complimenting his host. The stories of him getting sober after the better part of fifty years of living the life of a hard-driving and harder-partying musician appeared to be true.

For the moment, at least.

There were also rumblings circulating on the Internet that he was hitting the bottle again. At the moment, by all appearances, Derek was sober. If there was anything Darcy had learned in the months since she'd taken charge of Marysburg Music, it was to appreciate moments like this when all was well.

With her fingers crossed, she nodded to Hank. "Let's have some fun."

A buzz of excitement coursed through the store as fans streamed through the doorway to meet the man who'd performed onstage during history-making events from Newport Folk Fest to Live Aid to Burning Man. For Darcy, it was a moment of triumph. Derek was a true rock music legend, with five platinum albums, a dozen gold records, and twice as many awards to his name. He was, by far, the most famous celebrity Marysburg Music had ever hosted for an event.

And he'd personally asked Darcy to make it happen.

Her excitement was put on hold when a thin woman slid behind the sales counter into a spot next to her. The woman's short, platinum-blond hairstyle made Darcy think of singer Annie Lennox.

"I have to admit, I wasn't sure this was a good idea. I'm happy to be proven wrong."

"Just goes to show, you underestimate Marysburg, Indiana, at your peril, Vanessa." Darcy smiled as she took a moment to ring up a purchase by a young man who had been first in line. "What were you more worried about? The signing here or tonight's show?"

"To be honest, a little bit of both. As his tour manager, I thought Derek was crazy when he suggested making this first leg of the tour a big apology trip."

Darcy looked at the man who was the topic of their conversation. He was engaging with the fans, smiling and posing for selfies, and seemed to be having a genuinely good time. Shoot, even Char was grinning. And that was even after Darcy confessed to Char how the man had done so much to damage her drumming career.

"It meant a lot when he contacted me about doing this. I mean, first the apology to me over a video call, not some generic social media post, was nice. Then kicking off the tour here? In Marysburg? How could I say no to that?"

Vanessa raised her eyebrows. "Thank goodness you said yes. Once you forgave Derek, he got serious about rehearsing. He sounds good, and he's playing the best in thirty years. I've got high hopes for this tour."

The women exchanged high fives, then Darcy got busy ringing up sales. The up-tempo tunes from his Greatest Hits album helped keep the blood pumping and the fingers flying across the register keys. Before she knew it, Derek was getting to his feet, having signed a guitar for the last fan in line.

Even though she'd been too busy to step away from the register for even a moment, Darcy reveled in the festive vibe permeating the store. Derek took a selfie with Char and shared a joke with Hank. The legend even took a few minutes to chat with Darcy's high school-aged employees, Izzy and Peter. They'd dashed straight to the store the second school had let out for the day. The music legend hadn't disappointed them. He'd even gone as far as thanking them for the effort they made to come see him.

While Vanessa announced the winner of the concert tickets, Derek made his way toward the cash register. The plan had been for him to retreat to the office and leave via the back door, where a car was waiting for him.

"Darcy, love, would you be a dear and walk with me to the theater?" He put his hand on his heart. "I'd absolutely love to hear about the place before the sound check."

Unprepared for the sudden change of plans, Darcy went to her default answer. She started to say thanks, but she had a store to run. Before she could get the words out, Char was by her side. "She'd be honored, Mr. Tufnell. Go on, Darc. We've got it covered here. I'll tell the driver you all are walking."

The man clasped his hands together and broke into a grin that went from ear to ear. "Smashing. And Charlotte dear, it's Derek. Not any of that formality now that we're friends."

"In that case, I'd be delighted." Darcy beamed, because it was the truth.

With a spring in her step, Darcy accompanied Derek and Vanessa on the four-block walk from the record store to The Marysburg Center for the Performing Arts. On the way, Derek regaled her with stories from the wild days of his youth. Sex, drugs, and rock n roll, indeed.

"I'm way too old for that now, though. I haven't ingested any illegal substances in over eight years. I still like a glass of wine for a nightcap, but that's all. How awfully boring is that?" He let out a loud laugh. It was full of mirth and joy. "A few years ago, I even started doing yoga. Michael Franti convinced me to give it a go. It's one of the best decisions I've ever made. I feel twenty years younger, both mentally and physically."

Darcy shook her head. The last time she was in the company of this man, he'd been like a horrific, real-life version of Mr. Hyde. Now, he was as cuddly as Mr. Rogers.

They arrived at the Center for the Performing Arts to find a large, bearded man in a black jacket waiting for them.

"What's up, Chris?" Darcy gave the theater's manager, Chris Van Hoy, a hug as he waved them inside.

"We're ready for your soundcheck whenever you are, Mr. Tufnell." Chris gestured toward the stage. The rest of Derek's band and crew was assembled. They were busy tuning instruments and adjusting sound levels.

"Splendid." Derek rubbed his hands together. "Let's get to it, shall we?"

Vanessa's phone buzzed. After glancing at it, she put her hand on Derek's arm. The color had drained from her face. "There's someone waiting to see you in the green room."

"A surprise visitor. Well, let's all go see who it is. I think I can spare a moment or two." Derek waved for his manager to take the lead.

The woman weaved her way through the darkened theater, up a small flight of stairs, and through a short hall to the backstage area. It was an impressive demonstration of familiarity for someone who'd never been inside the building before today.

Curiosity niggled at Darcy as they approached the green room. Who was important enough to rate hanging out in the star's dressing room alone? And had the sway to get the man to delay his sound check, even for a short time? There'd been no mention of a special guest during the meet and greet, after all.

Her questions were nudged aside by a gold star affixed to the door at eye level. It had Derek's name written on it. The man was being given the royal treatment. The gesture made sense, though. Despite his record of boorish, and worse, behavior in the past, there was no doubt that Derek Tufnell was rock and roll royalty.

Darcy made a mental note to compliment Chris on the gesture. It was a nice touch.

With eyes wide like a kid gazing upon a pile of birthday presents, Derek opened the door. And came to a complete stop midway through the opening.

"Surprise, dear!" A woman with flame-red hair and dozens of spangly bracelets on her arms gave Derek a hug and kiss. She wore enough black eye shadow to make Alice Cooper jealous. And her strappy, five-inch stilettos looked like they'd come straight from the wardrobe of one of the Pussycat Dolls.

"Sophia, darling. This is an unexpected surprise." Derek waved Darcy and Vanessa into the dressing room as he grabbed a bottle of his flavored water from a mini-fridge next to a make-up desk. After introducing the woman to Darcy, he took three big gulps from the bottle. "To what do I owe the pleasure of your presence?"

"Didn't want to miss the start of your grand comeback tour. *Dear.*" The temperature in the room seemed to plummet thirty degrees, thanks to Sophia's icy glare. Apparently, this wasn't a good kind of surprise.

"That's so thoughtful of you," Vanessa said. "Why don't we let Derek get to his soundcheck, and then I can see how I can be of assistance to you."

"Oh, don't bother, Ms. Perez." Sophia slipped a black leather handbag featuring an interlocking GG symbol over her shoulder. "I'll find myself a spot to watch the soundcheck. From what I hear, it would be best if I keep an eye on him for a while."

"Whatever do you mean, my love?" Derek tugged at the sleeves of his shirt, unwilling or unable to make eye contact with his wife.

She let out a harsh laugh. "Don't play games with me. We're both too old for that. Ta."

Derek's cheeks bloomed flame red as Sophia exited the room by blowing him a kiss. Whatever was going on, it wasn't good.

And Darcy really didn't want to know about it. She had enough going on in her life. Getting caught up in someone else's domestic drama was not on her list.

"You know, I need to get back to the store." It sounded like an excellent way to extricate herself from an awkward situation. "Looking forward to the show tonight."

She was halfway down the hall when Vanessa caught up to her. Derek's manager held her hand out.

"Here are backstage passes for after the show. It's the least we can do after you've been such a gracious host. And," she nodded toward the dressing room, "after all that."

"That's very kind of you. I'm coming with two friends—"

"You're all welcome. See you tonight."

On her way back to the record store, Darcy pondered the weird exchange in the green room. It was strange on a couple of levels. First, Derek's wife seemed to surprise him by her visit. Then, her words and attitude were as cold as dry ice. With his wife acting so unfriendly, Darcy couldn't help wondering if the stories of the new Derek Tufnell, who'd cleaned up his act, were too good to be true.

After all, to have his spouse show up out of the blue and proceed to make the man as uncomfortable as a mouse cornered by Darcy's cat Ringo? That wasn't normal.

Then again, it seemed like Sophia knew something the rest of the world didn't. Like the recent rumors about his backsliding actually were true.

Judging by Vanessa's and Derek's reactions, they weren't happy with Sophia's gambit. Whatever it was, it sure looked like bad news for the musical legend.

Chapter Two

The excitement leading up to the show helped Darcy put the unsettling confrontation between Derek and Sophia out of her mind. The store was busy as concertgoers filled the aisles while the guitarist's music played over the speakers. It was a good day to be alive.

A few minutes after six o'clock, Darcy's day got even better. Liam Simmons strolled through Marysburg Music's entrance. He exchanged greetings with the store's employees, then leaned against the sales counter. "Ready to roll, Darc?"

"Ooh, is this like an official date?" Charlotte bounced up and down on her toes. She'd played a big part in Darcy and Liam's budding romantic relationship. Despite her and Izzy's encouragement, the pair were taking things slow. As in, snail's pace slow. Which was a pace that was way too dilatory to satisfy Char.

Liam scratched his forehead and turned toward Darcy. "Um. I mean…"

"He means it's not a date." Darcy rolled her eyes. "We're gonna grab Thea, get dinner, and take in the show. As friends. This night's too big of a deal to make Thea feel like a third wheel."

"Got to hand it to you, Boss." Peter joined the trio by the cash register. "After what that dude did to you, I don't see how you can be so nice to him."

"That's in the past, Peter. Derek asked for my forgiveness. I think his apology was sincere."

"Are you sure about that?" Hank crossed his arms. "I'm sorry, but a leopard can't change its spots. I don't want that man to hurt you ever again."

Izzy had been lingering in the vinyl section of the store where the rock albums were kept on display. Her gaze kept going back and forth between one of Derek's records and the group by the sales counter. It was as if she wanted to be part of the discussion, but didn't know how to join in.

"Wanna throw your two cents worth in, Iz?" Darcy smiled. It was important that everyone on the Marysburg Music team felt comfortable sharing what was on their mind.

The young woman let out a long sigh. "The man sexually harassed you, then told lies about you. It doesn't get much worse than that." She put up her index finger to keep anyone from cutting in. "But, if you could forgive him, that's good enough for me and should be good enough for everyone else. I mean, doing all this stuff here in Marysburg shows a lot of sincerity to me."

"And this is why I love you all. We may not always agree, but the fact that every one of you has my back means a ton. Seriously. And I've got yours, too."

"Does that include me?" A young man with wavy, shoulder-length hair placed a Primus album on the counter.

"You keep buying my prog rock, Ace, I'll have your back until the day I die." She rang up the sale for the man, who was a regular customer. "And, now, Liam and I are out of here."

They kept the conversation light on their walk to pick up Thea at her place of employment, Selena's Mexican Restaurant and Cantina. Mostly, Liam asked about Derek's music. Darcy loved the man, who was her best friend, but the fact that he didn't listen to any music created before the twenty-first century was a constant source of annoyance.

He was missing out on so much amazing music. From the era of Glenn Miller and big band swing to Patsy Cline and traditional country to the raging punk rock of The Clash, the twentieth century produced an absolute treasure trove of music of all types. Well, if he was unwilling to change, it was his loss.

The moment they stepped into Selena's bar area, Thea practically leapt from her workstation to join them. The woman, over six foot tall and a couple hundred pounds of lean muscle, had the grace of a ballet dancer despite her rugby-playing build.

"Give me two seconds, dudes. I need to go change." She sprinted toward the restrooms with a black T-shirt in one hand.

"Ten bucks says that's a Derek Tufnell shirt she's changing into," Liam said.

"You're on. I think she'll be representing her favorite music store, the one and only Marysburg Music."

When Thea emerged from the restroom, the shirt she was wearing was emblazoned with the logo from Derek's infamous 1978 "Whiskey and Horsepower" Tour. Liam nudged Darcy with his elbow and put out his hand.

"Whatever." Darcy slapped a twenty onto his open palm. "That's all I got. I'll expect change after you get the first round of drinks at the show."

"What's that about?" Thea tossed her work shirt to a co-worker behind the bar, then slipped her arms through Darcy's and Liam's and guided them out of the restaurant.

"Just a little wager on who you were representing tonight. The featured artist or your favorite music store." Darcy bumped her shoulder against Thea's upper arm. "I lost. You traitor."

"Come on, D. That's not fair. Derek Tufnell, The Guitar Slinger himself, is my favorite musician of all time. Betting against him tonight was like betting against the house in Vegas."

"I know." Once they were outside, Darcy flipped up the collar of her jacket to ward off the chill in the October air. "And the house always wins."

"Or, in this case, I win." Liam let out a laugh, then jogged ahead of them. "Oh, look, there's the restaurant. Let me be a gentleman and get the door for you ladies."

Thea looked from Liam's sprinting form to Darcy. She shrugged. "Sometimes, he's a big dork, but you could do worse."

"Yeah, well, it kind of depends on how fast he gives me the ten bucks he owes me. By the way, I got these little beauties this afternoon." She handed the backstage passes to Thea. "Think you can stick around after the show to meet your idol?"

After staring at the laminated passes for several seconds, she wrapped Darcy up in a bone-crushing hug. "This is turning into the greatest night of my life. You're amazing, D."

It was Darcy's turn to laugh. "Totally my pleasure. Do me a favor, though. You know how you just said I was amazing? Would you mind saying it again? This time, in front of Liam."

"Tonight, anything for you, girl."

After an amazing dinner of Caesar salads followed by deep-dish pizza, the trio made the three-block walk to the theater.

"This is going to be so amazing." Thea was a ball of excited energy as they joined the queue to enter the Marysburg Center for the Performing Arts. "Dinner, reserved seats, and backstage passes. Talk about a night I'll never forget."

"Since I've never seen Derek before," Liam said as they inched forward. "What do you think the show will be like?"

Darcy opened her mouth, but Thea beat her to the punch. "From what I've heard, he'll play his hits, but some supposedly have new arrangements. Rumor has it that he's going to debut some new music, too."

"Okay. New music. I can get behind that." Liam looked around at the boisterous crowd and nodded.

Darcy shook her head. "Says the guy who only came because I promised to pick up the tab for dinner. Trust me, dude. Your life will never be the same after tonight."

If only Darcy had known how prophetic that statement would turn out to be.

* * *

The stage lights dimmed at eight, sharp. Derek wasn't touring with an opening act. He'd confided in Darcy that he wanted to prove to himself, his fans, and his critics that he still had it. That meant a two-hour show plus another fifteen-minute encore.

The man did not disappoint. After stumbling over a power cable walking to his microphone, he opened the show with a solo, acoustic version of the song he wrote mourning the loss of his first wife, "Miss You, Baby." Before the crowd finished their applause, his band joined him onstage, and they ripped into a blues-soaked version of his biggest hit, "Dragstrip to Nowhere." The hits kept coming and only let up during the break between the main set and when the band returned to the stage for the encore.

"I've got a new tune for you. I hope you don't mind letting this old warhorse try it out on you." The song started with a standard twelve-bar blues riff, then morphed into a New Orleans-style jazzy, syncopated beat that had the crowd, which had been on its feet all night, dancing in the aisles.

"Check it out." Darcy had to shout to Thea to be heard. She pointed at Liam, who was doing a mash-up of the swim and the robot. "Looks like we've got ourselves a convert."

"Amen, sister." The women exchanged a high five and joined their friend by busting out their own moves.

A little while later, the show came to a rousing end with a cover version of one of Pixie Dust's biggest hits, "Let's Ride." While the rest of the crowd jammed along to the rough and ready anthem to life on the road, it was all Darcy could do to hold back the tears. To hear a rock and roll legend perform a song she wrote for her own band, before a live audience no less, left her breathless.

Not a soul among the assembled throng moved toward the exits until the house lights came up. It was as if there was a communal hope that if everyone stuck around, Derek would take the stage yet again. Darcy sipped on a ginger ale as she soaked in the scene. Her head was spinning from the fact that the amazing show even included one of her songs.

It had been a fabulous performance. A once in a lifetime experience. If Derek was serious about a comeback, he'd be playing to sold-out shows across North America and back home in the UK in no time.

"You miss this at all?" Liam put his arm around her. The gesture had a more of a friend vibe than a boyfriend vibe. Still, it felt good. "Especially after him playing a Dust song. I mean, wow. Did you know about that?"

"I don't know. I miss it a little, maybe." She took another sip of her drink. "I miss the energy I got from the crowd when we were up there on stage. I don't miss the mind-numbing hours on the road and the cramped living arrangements. Still, having someone cover a song you wrote never gets old."

"You sound like you're at peace with that part of your life in the past."

"I am. I wouldn't be here if I hadn't gone through all that." Darcy glanced at Thea, who had returned to them after a trip to the merch stand. "Ready to meet the man, himself?"

She held out her haul, which included a T-shirt, tank top, sticker, and concert poster. "More than you imagine."

With a grin that matched her ebullient mood, Darcy led the trio to the backstage area. She left it to Thea to flash the passes. While Darcy had performed with Derek and knew him on a first-name basis, Thea was a way bigger fan of the man's music. The kind-hearted bartender deserved to get as much out of the night's experience as possible.

The door to the green room was open. Derek was seated on the couch with a towel in one hand and yet another bottle of his flavored water in the other. Vanessa was at his side, looking at something on her tablet. A short and thin bald man had his back to the far wall. Despite the stuffy post-concert conditions in the room, he looked totally at ease in a hound's tooth pattern blazer and plaid scarf.

Derek got to his feet when Darcy knocked on the door frame. He had to use the couch arm to steady himself as he stood.

"And here she is. Tonight's guardian angel." He took Darcy's hands in his and gave them a squeeze. "Did you enjoy the show?"

Her cheeks got hot at being the center of attention. It was something she was working on. As the owner of Marysburg Music, she was the face of the store. Whether she wanted to be or not. Her predecessor, Eddie Maxwell, had been an entertainer at heart and reveled in meeting people and making new friends. Darcy was much more reserved than her mentor had been, but she was making progress.

"It was amazing." She introduced Liam and Thea. The thin man was Brian McGuinness, Derek's producer. "Thank you so much for a night we'll never forget."

"You are so amazing," Thea blurted out. "Can I get your autograph?"

"My pleasure, love." Derek chuckled at the armload of items the woman held out. Then he swayed on his feet for a moment and dropped back onto the couch. "I guess the performance took more out of me than I thought. Why don't you take a seat next to me."

Darcy's attention was drawn to an award that was sitting on an end table below a flat-screen TV. A gold-plated, old-fashioned record player, complete with a megaphone, sat atop a shiny black base. It wasn't large. Darcy could hold it in one hand with ease.

Its significance was enormous, though.

"Blues Album of the year. Nineteen, Eighty-Nine." She showed the Grammy to Liam. "The year I was born."

"In that case, we must have a picture. I always tour with one or two awards. They serve as reminders to put all I can into each show. Just like I put all I could into my records that won awards." Derek finished signing Thea's items and, once again, struggled to get up. It took him three tries to get to his feet. "If I didn't know better, I'd think I'd just had a wee spot of whiskey."

Brian helped him. "We're not as young as we used to be. And that was your first full-length show in a while."

"Of course." Derek flashed his legendary smile. Thea almost swooned right in front of everyone. "Let's take that snap."

When the photos had been taken to Thea's satisfaction, Derek gave Darcy a long hug.

"If you don't mind, I'd like a moment alone with the lovely Ms. Gaughan." His cheeks pinked up. "To express my gratitude for her forgiveness and recent support."

Liam shot Darcy a glance with raised eyebrows. She returned the look with a quick shake of her head. Tonight, Derek wasn't a threat. Not like that horrific night eight years ago.

"Vanessa, why don't we introduce our new friends to the band?" Brian opened his arms wide to usher the folks out of the room until it was only Darcy and Derek.

The guitar legend closed the door, then took a deep breath.

"I wanted to thank you again for all of your kindness and understanding. More importantly, I want to apologize in person for mistreating you the way

I did after that set in Louisville. I should never have done that, period. End of story. If I could, I'd go back in time and fix things so that never happened."

A knot formed in Darcy's stomach as terrible memories of that night came flooding back. Among countless bad nights from that era, it stood out as the worst.

Even worse than the night she was kicked out of Pixie Dust, the band she'd founded.

She swallowed to get past a lump that had formed in her throat. Her right hand started a rhythmic thrumming on her leg. It was one of her classic signs of anxiety. After a couple of deep breaths, the lump cleared, and her fingers stopped.

"Thank you, Derek. I'm thankful that you've come to realize how despicable your behavior was. I also appreciate the efforts you've made in acknowledging how wrong it was. I imagine it wasn't easy to make that public apology to me and all the other women you hurt, but you did it. Like I said before, I believe your sincerity. And I forgive you."

"I don't deserve your kindness, Darcy." He wiped his brow as he plopped back onto the couch. His face had become flushed. "Whew. I guess the show took more out of me than I expected."

She sat next to him. "It's not easy looking yourself in the mirror and admitting the wrongs you've done to others. It's even harder doing it face to face." She chuckled. "Believe me, I know. Taking the time to make your apologies in person is a good thing, Derek."

"Will it get easier?"

"I don't know. You wronged a lot of women, and each of them has to carry what you did with them. My guess is that every time you make an apology, it'll be tough. Don't forget about the good it will be doing, though. Both for you and the people you'll be making amends to."

"Well, thank you again. I'll remember this talk." He closed his eyes as he leaned his head back. "What a day. I think I'm going to meditate for a wee bit. Be good to yourself, Darcy."

"You, too." She gave his hand a friendly squeeze and got to her feet. "And I am so grateful to you for playing "Let's Ride." You totally nailed it. Good luck with the rest of the tour. I'm sure it's going to be totally lights out."

In the hall, she crossed paths with Hamilton "Hambone" Barclay, Derek's keyboard player and long-time collaborator. The guitarist, Drew Easton, was at his side.

"Enjoy the show?" Hambone had a towel draped around his neck. The perspiration that was still on his brow proved Derek wasn't the only one who'd gotten in a good workout while onstage. Drew, on the other hand, hadn't broken a sweat.

"Very much. Thanks. I just had a really nice visit with Derek, too. He's in the green room meditating if you need to talk to him."

"Nah." Drew shook his head. "Don't want to interrupt him. He deserves the breather. We can always debrief on the bus."

"Where are you performing next?" Darcy had been so wrapped up in Derek's appearance in Marysburg she hadn't paid attention to where else the band was scheduled to perform.

"Columbus, Ohio, tomorrow night." The keyboard player leaned against the wall. "Then we have two days off before we play Lexington, Kentucky. We're keeping the back-to-back appearances to a minimum. Derek and I aren't as young as we used to be."

"None of us are." Darcy grinned, then exchanged fist bumps with the musicians. "Well, again, great show and safe travels."

A little while later, Darcy, Liam, and Thea were back out in front of the theater. Thea was taking a selfie in front of the marquee.

"What a night, huh?" Darcy leaned against Liam. In her hands, she held a concert poster Derek had autographed. She was going to frame it and put it up at the record store.

"Unforgettable. Thea and I are going to grab a beer at Selena's. She said she was too wired from the show to go home. Want to join us?"

"Nah, I'm good." Darcy glanced at her phone. It was a little after eleven. "I'm gonna drop this off at the store. I have a few things I need to do since I left early. Text me tomorrow. I know a place where you can get a bunch of records by your new favorite artist."

They parted with hugs and good-natured ribbing of Thea for all the merch she bought. The brisk October night invigorated Darcy as she strolled to the record store. Even the discordant noise of workers tossing trash into the theater's dumpster couldn't mar the event. She marveled at Derek's high energy level throughout the show. The man was in his early seventies but had better endurance than her.

Until after the show.

"Probably low blood sugar." She nodded and pulled out her key to the store. That must have been it. His fancy flavored water may have contained a lot of bubbles, but not much else nutrient-wise.

Once inside the store, she laid the poster out on the counter and put some albums on top of it to speed the flattening process. Then she reviewed the day's sales receipts. She smiled and practically skipped to the spot where Derek's albums were normally slotted, between the eighties band 'Til Tuesday and long-time Indiana blues favorite Duke Tumatoe.

The space was empty.

The situation was the same in the CD section.

In the mood to take advantage of the concert, which would no doubt be getting rave reviews, she fired up the computer in her office. There was no better time to replenish the stock of Derek Tufnell music.

She'd just hit "Send" on an order of a dozen albums and three CDs from Derek's discography, along with a few Dire Straits records and the latest from up-and-coming Blues wizard Christone "Kingfish" Ingram, when there was an insistent hammering on the store's front door. It wasn't unusual for kids looking for some low-level trouble or someone who'd had one too many adult beverages to wander through the Marysburg Business District after dark, banging on windows and making a nuisance of themselves.

Darcy ignored it. Shoot, she'd been known to do it herself back in the day.

When the hammering returned, this time at a volume that had been turned up to eleven, Darcy went to see what all the fuss was about. While she didn't believe in violence, she did grab a baseball bat on the way to the front of the store.

Couldn't hurt to be on the safe side.

"The store's closed. We'll be open tomorrow at ten."

The shadowy figure on the other side of the glass didn't move on. She raised her voice and repeated the statement while brandishing the bat.

"I said—"

"And I heard you the first time." The visitor held up something shiny close to the window. It was silver and somewhat oblong in shape, tapering to a pointed end at the bottom.

It was a badge worn by members of the Marysburg Police Department.

"It's Detective-Sergeant Rosengarten, Ms. Gaughan. Open the door. I need to talk to you."

Darcy's blood ran cold. If there was a bane to her existence, it was Kaitlin Rosengarten. The two had a long and difficult history but had only crossed paths once in recent years. That had been six months ago, when the Detective-Sergeant was investigating the murder of Darcy's boss.

In the end, it was Darcy who solved the case. Not the police.

If that same police officer was literally banging on her door at midnight, it couldn't be good.

With a cold sweat forming on her brow, Darcy unlocked the door and waved Kaitlin inside. "What can I do for you, Detective-Sergeant?"

"There's been an incident. I stopped by your house and didn't find you there, so I thought I'd try seeing if you were here. Can you tell me where you've been the last two hours?" The woman widened her stance as she flipped to a page in her notebook. If Darcy was going to make a run for it, it would have to be through Kaitlin.

Not that Darcy had any plans to run. She had no reason to.

"I was at the Derek Tufnell show with Liam and Thea. It ended about ten-thirty, and then we spent some time with Derek backstage." She showed Kaitlin the backstage pass, which had been in the back pocket of her jeans. "After that, I came here to do some work. Why?"

"Do you make a habit of going to work after a late night out with friends?"

That's a weird question. Darcy shook off the combative thought. It wouldn't do her any good to get into a battle of words with the police officer.

"Not usually, no." She told Kaitlin about Thea and Liam going for a beer. "I wanted to drop off the poster Derek signed. While I was here, I saw that we sold out of his music, so I stuck around to order more."

"And none of that could wait until morning."

"I suppose, sure. I needed to come by anyway, though. My jeep's parked in the back." Darcy gritted her teeth. Now that the high from the show was wearing off, weariness was kicking in. "What's all this about?"

"At eleven, fifteen, Derek Tufnell was found unresponsive in his dressing room. He's dead."

"What?" Darcy grabbed onto one of the record bins to steady herself. "That can't be. He was fine when I left him. Any idea how he died?"

"Does this photo mean anything to you?" The officer showed her phone to Darcy. It was a shot of Darcy and Derek together, holding the Grammy award. They both had big grins, as if neither had a care in the world.

"Yeah. Derek's manager took that. I've got that same picture on my phone. Liam took it for me. Why?"

"Mr. Tufnell was murdered. Someone hit him over the head with that award. And by all accounts, you were the last person to see him alive."

Chapter Three

"No way. That can't be." Darcy recounted her conversation with Derek. "When I left him, he was fine. Looked tired, but that was it. And the award was on the table by the TV, not bashed into his head."

"So, you admit to being alone with him." Kaitlin gave her a long, unblinking stare, like a lion about pounce on its prey. "After this photo was taken."

"Yeah, for maybe five minutes. He wanted to have a private chat with me. You can ask anyone who was there." She fought against the shakiness in her voice. The conversation seemed to be headed south, so she decided to take control.

"First off, Derek was alive and well when we parted ways. Second, if I was going to kill him, why would I incriminate myself by using something I'd just had my picture taken with? I know you don't like me, but give me some credit. I'm not that dumb."

"Point taken." Kaitlin's phone buzzed. "I have to go conduct some preliminary interviews. Mr. Tufnell's band and crew have agreed to stay in town for a few days while we investigate. It's not like they have to be anywhere now. You should stick around, too."

She nodded and headed back outside. The conversation had taken less than five minutes. It had turned Darcy's world upside down.

And not the good way like in the classic "Upside Down" by Diana Ross.

For a second, she thought about dialing Liam. While she was considering her options, a notification on her phone went off. She'd been tagged in a social media post.

It was from Thea. She'd shared two photos she took during the visit backstage. One of them was of Derek with his arm around her. The other had added Darcy and Liam to the mix. The caption made Darcy want to smile and cry at the same time.

"Got to meet my favorite guitarist EVA, Derek Tufnell!!! One of the best nights of my life with my best buds!!!"

Darcy looked at the poster of Jason Isbell on the wall. "Good golly, Miss Molly. What am I going to do? You know a little bit about sad songs. Got any suggestions for me?"

Jason didn't respond, which was for the best. If he had said something, even if it was the best advice in the history of the planet, she would have worried she'd lost her marbles once and for all.

Instead, she thought about her behavioral health toolbox, which contained strategies for coping with stressful and emotional situations. It sat in a corner of her mind, dusty from lack of use in recent months. But always available when needed.

And, boy, did she need it right then.

She went back to the office and, once seated, closed her eyes and took long, cleansing breaths. In through the nose. Then out through the mouth. For ten minutes, her body's only movements involved her mouth, nose, and the steady rising and falling of her chest.

At the end of the meditation session, she opened her eyes. The world was still in place. More importantly, Darcy knew what to do.

"One minute, one hour, one day at a time." She draped a messenger bag that served as a purse over her shoulder and headed out the door. The first order of business was to take care of herself and her cat, Ringo. After a good night's sleep, she'd figure out what to do about the devastating news.

"Hey, buddy. I'm home." Darcy scooped Ringo up into her arms. The cat responded with a *mrrh* to indicate his displeasure at her late arrival home but let her scratch him behind an ear. "It was the best night ever until it wasn't."

She set her feline buddy down and told him about the evening while she made him a dinner of fancy, wet food. It was the least she could do since she'd been out so late. While Ringo attacked his feast, Darcy added water to the little fountain he drank from, then cleaned out his litter box. The glamorous life of a cat owner.

She wouldn't have it any other way.

When her cat mom tasks were finished, she brewed a cup of herbal tea and got comfortable in her recliner. Ringo joined her once she put her feet up.

"What am I gonna do?" Too worked up to sleep, she began scrolling through social media on her phone. There were dozens of posts mentioning Derek and the concert. The older ones focused on the show and how excited fans were to have the guitar legend back out on the road.

A few of the more recent posts were troubling. Apparently, word about Derek's untimely death had gotten out. Words like "murder" and "suicide" were being thrown about like so many guitar picks thrown from the stage at a concert. There was no comment from Marysburg PD, but Darcy couldn't help but wonder who let that cat out of the bag.

And even more upsetting, why?

By the time she finished the doom-scrolling session, Ringo was fast asleep, snoring away on her lap. After the past two hours of awfulness and negativity, she couldn't bear to disturb her fur baby. Instead, she gave him another round of ear scratches, turned off the light, and fell asleep in the chair.

* * *

When the alarm went off, signaling Saturday morning's arrival, she was still in the recliner. Ringo was absent. She found him a moment later, curled up dead center in the middle of the bed, his face hidden by his tail.

"Oh, I see how it is." She rubbed the small of her back. It was a little stiff. "You could have told me when you got up. Now I need an extra-long, hot shower to get the kinks out."

The cat ignored her. Which wasn't a surprise. He tended to do that when she had the audacity to reprimand him about something.

By the time she finished showering, her phone was blowing up with notifications faster than tickets were sold for Taylor Swift's most recent tour. She forced herself to ignore it until she was dressed and had a mug of tea brewing. There was only so much she could do at this point.

The sheer volume of texts and other messages ruined any appetite she may have had, so she munched on a plain English muffin while she went through them. She'd respond based on relative importance. Anything she was tagged in on social media could wait. Messages from friends and family were the priority.

First, she made calls to her mom and sister, assuring them she was okay. Before she ended the calls, she promised them she'd keep them in the loop as the investigation progressed. Returning a voicemail message from Thea, who sounded like she was in tears, was next on the list.

"Holy cow, D. Is it really true?" Thea had cut straight to the heart of the matter the second she answered.

"Afraid so. Kaitlin Rosengarten came by the store late last night to give me the news." While it wasn't exactly the truth, it wouldn't help to dump the details of the conversation on her grieving friend. While Thea looked as tough as a dragon, she was as soft and cuddly as a newborn kitten with friends and family.

She choked back tears, then blew her nose.

"I can't believe it. The murderer must have been hanging around the same time we were." She took in a deep breath. "Did Rosengarten say if they have any suspects or leads?"

Yeah, me. Darcy kept the snarky response to herself. Saying it out loud wouldn't help Thea's state of mind. Instead, she kept it vague.

"They're looking into a few things. It's going to be okay, T."

"A few things. Right. You and I both know how that worked out the last time something like this went down," Thea growled. "You have to investigate this, D. Like last time."

Darcy almost dropped her phone. "You can't be serious. Last time was different. Eddie saved my life. I owed him."

"I get that. Will you do it for me, then? I grew up listening to Derek's music. Meeting him last night was one of the highlights of my life. Seriously."

Marysburg, Indiana, had a population in the neighborhood of ten thousand souls. Of those, Darcy could literally count on one hand the number of those souls who'd been there for her when she'd been at her lowest. Thea was among that small group.

She couldn't say no to her friend.

"I'll do what I can. I gotta be honest, though. I don't know how much that will be."

"It'll be enough."

They chatted for a bit, then Darcy ended the call. She drummed her fingers on the table. A night's rest had cooled her anger toward the Detective-Sergeant somewhat. Despite the fact she'd just promised Thea she'd look into the murder, there was no denying following through on that commitment could open a lot of dangerous doors. To her emotional well-being every bit as much as her physical health.

What was the right thing to do? Keeping to the sideline and letting the police do their jobs was the logical, sensible choice. Darcy had made a promise, though. She and Eddie had spent many nights talking about the importance of being a woman of her word. Becoming someone her friends could rely on. She'd made a commitment. There was no turning back now.

She had to get to work. In more ways than one.

On her way out the door, she tossed Ringo a few kitty treats. "Later, skater. Looks like I'm gonna be doing the private eye thing again. I'd appreciate any kitty thoughts and prayers you want to send my way."

Central Indiana weather in mid-October was a lot like the line-up at a music festival. Sometimes, it was amazing and memory-making. Other times, it leaned toward dull and forgettable. Regardless, it was never predictable.

With the sun shining through a smattering of wispy clouds, the day looked like it was going to land closer to the amazing category. Darcy grabbed her skateboard from the storage area of her jeep, which she affectionately called Rusty, and set off to work using only her legs for power.

In a turn of good fortune, a year after Darcy bought the fishing cabin she called home, the city built a paved bike path that ended at a boat launch a couple hundred yards from her house. The path had turned out to be another of the many bright spots that came with living in a home situated at the confluence of Mary's Creek and the White River.

The four-mile trek took her alongside the river into the Marysburg business district. At Harrison Street, the main north-to-south drag, she turned left and made her way up a slight incline to River Road. From there, it was only a few blocks until she arrived at her destination.

Marysburg Music.

It didn't matter how many times she skateboarded to work. Every trip was time well spent. The fresh air invigorated her. The exercise helped her stay in shape. And minutes on the board gave her time to think.

More often than not, she thought about the store. What records she needed to buy, what acts to vet for the Wednesday and Saturday open mic events, what she could do to help Izzy get into the Ball State School of Music.

On this morning, with each push of her leg, she went deeper and deeper into thought about who, or what had brought about Derek's untimely death. It was a conundrum. The man seemed in good spirits, if tired, at the end of the show. His days of drinking and womanizing were behind him. Well, maybe they were. Sure, he was in his seventies, but the days he had left seemed to be bright.

Shoot, Darcy had seen B.B. King play a show in Indianapolis when the King of the Blues was in his mid-eighties. Mick Jagger was still prancing around massive stages for the Rolling Stones in his late seventies. There was no reason to expect Derek's life would be cut short in such a sudden and violent manner.

When the familiar purple and red Marysburg Music marquee came into view, she set her musings aside to focus on what she was going to say to her team and folks who came into the store.

Hank and Peter were scheduled for the early shift. They both knew she'd been at the concert. The older man was as perceptive as he was kind. She had faith that he'd take his cues from her. The younger one would want as many details as she'd be willing to share. God love him, Peter hadn't developed much of a filter yet.

Which was going to pose a challenge, given the visit from the police fewer than twelve hours before.

"Just be honest. They trust you." She gave the skateboard a final push. "You've worked to earn that trust. Now's not the time to lose it."

It was still fifteen minutes before opening time when Darcy entered the store.

"Morning." Hank waved at her from behind the sales counter, where he'd been cleaning the glass. "Quite the night, huh?"

"That's putting it mildly." She extended her arm and slapped her palms as she walked by on her way to the office. Since he'd broached the subject, it was pointless to avoid it. "What have you heard."

"That it was an amazing show. That Derek Tufnell sounded good and played even better."

She shoved her messenger bag into a drawer in her desk and turned to find Hank had followed her. "True on both counts. Since you came all the way back here, that's not all, I'm assuming."

"No, it's not, unfortunately." He removed his glasses and wiped the lenses with a cloth. "I've also heard that Derek was murdered after the show. And you, my friend, seem to be a suspect."

"Yeah, it's so sad." She headed for the doorway but stopped mid-step. "Wait a minute. Did you say I'm a suspect?"

Hank put up his hands. "I didn't say that. Folks on social media are, though. The official word from the cops is that they're conducting the investigation, and haven't formed any conclusions yet, blah, blah, blah. Word is apparently circulating, though. Your name's been leaked as a suspect."

Darcy wanted to scream, pound a drumhead until it broke, track down Kaitlin and strangle her. None of those things would solve the mystery, though. Instead, she let out a low growl. That went on for a several seconds. Then she told Hank about the Detective-Sergeant's late-night visit.

"If it was anybody but her, I wouldn't believe it. What that woman has against you is beyond me."

She put her arm around Hank and led him back to the sales floor. It was almost time to open for the day. Not unlike a few months ago, a murder investigation couldn't be allowed to get in the way of Marysburg Music doing business.

The record store was Darcy's livelihood. It was also the main source of income for Hank and Charlotte. Even though Peter and Izzy were in high school, and could probably find another job in no time, they were part of Marysburg Music.

Darcy had a lot of people depending on her. She wouldn't let them down by letting the store suffer. She'd done it before. She could do it again. Despite the obstacles that she might find along the way, Darcy Gaughan was capable of doing two things at once.

"She's probably trying to scare me. No matter what, when she looks at me, she sees the wreck I used to be, not the person I am now. I guess she's not ready to give me the benefit of the doubt yet."

Hank went back behind the counter while Darcy headed toward the front window to turn on the "Open" sign.

"It seems to me that she thinks you showed her up in the spring. Not that I'm defending her, but going from a thorn in her side to catching a murderer before she did can't sit well with her."

Hank's honesty while paying her a compliment warmed Darcy's heart. The man was a steady source of solid, fatherly advice. It often came in handy since her parents lived three hours away and didn't always have time in the middle of the day to hash out a problem.

"You speak the truth. Which is why, once again, I'm going to become a whole rose bush full of thorns in her side." She unlocked the door. "Because I've decided. I'm going to figure out who murdered Derek."

Chapter Four

They had put the conversation on hold as customers streamed into the store as soon as Darcy opened the door. Some of the traffic was due to the regular Saturday shopping crowd. A small group consisted of folks wanting to get their hands on anything Derek related. The final portion, and the chattiest by far, was made up of friends of the store who were trying to cope with the horrible news and wanted to gather with others dealing with the same emotions.

As soon as Peter arrived, she assigned him to make sure the coffee station was kept fully stocked. It was no small assignment, given how busy the store was. And how many people wanted to hang out and commiserate.

"Seriously, Boss?" He frowned, a gesture one saw from Peter about as often as Metallica released a love song. "If I wanted to be a barista, I'd go work at the Big Bean."

The young man was hurting. Fewer than twenty-four hours before, he'd met his first musical superstar. Now that man was dead. Peter's surly response was no doubt a sign of his struggle to cope. She couldn't hold that against him.

Instead, she put her arm around him.

"Today, people are going to come here to mourn as much as to buy. We need to make sure they feel welcome to do that. Keeping the coffee station full and tidy will help with that. In return, you can choose the music today."

"I guess." He stared at the tile floor and tapped it with the toe of his checkered flag Vans shoe. "Can we play Derek all day?"

The question was a punch to Darcy's solar plexus. She wasn't ready to hear the man's music. Not yet. Her state of personal grief was still lodged largely in the avoidance category. Listening to the man would only make his premature departure all the more real.

But this moment wasn't about her.

It was about the Marysburg Music community. On this day, a lot of them were hurting. If Derek's music helped them get through the day, it was the least she could do.

"Yep." She hugged him. "Hit it."

"Yesi." He laughed at the reference to the tagline of Captain Chris Pike from the *Star Trek, Strange New Worlds* series. Pretty much everyone who knew Darcy was well aware of her crush on Anson Mount, the actor who played Captain Pike. She never passed on a chance to quote him.

A while later, Todd Robinson, one of the store's best customers and an all-around good guy, approached her. His eyes were red-rimmed, and his shoulders sagged with each ragged breath he took.

"I was at the show with some friends." He took a sip from his cup of coffee. There was no need to specify what show. "We had a great time, and then to find out…." He got too choked up to finish.

She put her arms around him and held him as he sobbed. Todd was a kind soul who wore his emotions on his sleeve. He loved the store and felt its highest of highs and lowest of lows as if he was the owner.

"Whoever did this won't get away with it. I promise." She gave him a squeeze. A little flame of confidence kindled to life inside her. Yes, she'd made a promise. And she was a woman of her word.

"You gonna ride to the rescue like you did with Eddie's case?"

"I don't know about that. The first step is clearing my name. After the reception y'all gave me at the end of that one, it was kind of nice to feel like a superhero. Hate to have my perfect record tarnished, though."

The man chuckled. "Everyone here's got your back. If you decide to get involved again."

"More like when." Peter extended his fist toward Darcy. When she bumped it, he exchanged a high-five with Todd. "You don't mess with the Boss Lady."

"One day at a time, guys." Afraid of raising expectations, she excused herself, saying she needed to check something in the office.

Upon her arrival, a startling scene was awaiting her. Hank was hanging the store's spare whiteboard on the wall. The words "suspect, motive, means, opportunity" had been written across the top in blue ink.

"Izzy got here a few minutes ago. Thought I'd give you a head start on your investigation." He handed a dry-erase marker to her. "No time like the present."

"Alrighty, then." She tapped the marker against her thigh. "If anyone asks, I'm scheduling appointments to look at record collections to buy. The world doesn't need to know what I'm doing. Not yet."

"As you wish." He bowed to her and left her alone with her thoughts.

And the case board.

In no time, she had a decent list of suspects-Derek's band members, the two technicians, Producer Paul, Road Manager Vanessa, and his wife Sophia. She didn't have anything in terms of motive and means, but it was a start. She tossed the marker on the desk when there was a knock on the door.

Izzy opened the door just wide enough to poke her head in. "Sorry to bug you, Darcy, but...."

The young woman's gaze went to the board. After a moment, she slipped inside, closing the door behind her.

"How can I help?"

"No. I'm not dragging you or Peter into this. You both have enough going on between school and your college applications." She moved toward the door, but Izzy cut her off.

"You know people online are saying you did it, right? That makes it personal. Nobody messes with our boss."

Darcy let out a little laugh. God love her, Izzy was becoming a strong, independent woman. She didn't want to crush that. Women should lift each other up, right? Right.

"Fine. Keep your eyes on social media. If you or Peter notice something interesting, flag it somehow, and we can talk about it. That's all, though. Deal?"

"Sure. For now." She stepped aside. "Before you head out there, that detective is here. She said she wants to talk to you."

"Good golly, Miss Molly, what now?" Darcy pulled her hair into a side ponytail. It was an attempt to channel her inner Rachael Price, the singer from the band Lake Street Dive. The style choice was a nod to the song "Side Pony" that talked about living one's life on their own terms.

Times were tough right now. Darcy was tough, too. She was determined to stand tall in the face of her law enforcement adversary.

"Detective-Sergeant, good afternoon." Darcy walked straight up to the cop with a confident stride and extended her hand. "How can I help you?"

"I see you're a lot busier now than when we last spoke." Her stone-faced stare was unreadable. The kind a poker player would love to have.

"Saturday's our busiest day of the week." She nodded toward the coffee station. "Today, a lot of Derek Tufnell fans have come to hang out together. Some are here to mourn, others to celebrate his life. Regardless of the reason, they're part of the Marysburg Music community and welcome to hang out as long as they want."

"Yeah, I've heard people talk about the community thing you've got here."

The cop's dismissive tone and use of air quotes around "community" grated on Darcy's nerves. She took a breath and counted to five before responding. In the back of her mind, she couldn't help wondering if her nemesis was goading her into saying something regrettable or was simply not a nice person.

"I know you're super busy, Detective-Sergeant. What's going on?"

"We have more questions about Derek Tufnell. I need you to come to the station to answer them."

Darcy made a point of looking around the room. It was bursting with motion and sound and a palpable energy. It wasn't an environment to leave her team short-handed.

"Can't we talk in my office? I really should be here in case somebody needs me."

"I'm afraid not." The cop widened her stance and put her hands on her hips. "You can come willingly, or you can make a scene. It's up to you."

You'd love for me to make a scene. That way, you can cuff me and make me

31

look like the bad guy. Sorry. Not going to give you the satisfaction. The thought crossed Darcy's mind in the blink of an eye. It brought forth a smile. In the past, she would have reacted in a way that gave Kaitlin all the power.

Those days were gone.

"Hey, Hank." She waved at the man, who was busy ringing up sales. "The Detective-Sergeant needs my help at the station with some things pertaining to last night. Hold down the fort, will you?"

"You got it, Boss." The man's mouth curled up on one end. He understood Darcy's message on both a literal level as well as the meaning between the words. "See you soon."

It came as totally no surprise to Darcy that Kaitlin was as quiet as downtown Marysburg at three A.M. during the five-minute trip to police headquarters. Once they arrived, she was only slightly more communicative, with a terse "come with me" followed by a slam of the police cruiser's driver door.

The women went straight to an interview room, with Kaitlin only slowing down enough to grab a file folder and a pen from her desk. When a couple of folks in the office waved at Darcy, she returned the gestures with a smile.

Kaitlin notwithstanding, Darcy's cred with the Marysburg PD had rocketed to the top of the charts in the aftermath of the Eddie Maxwell case. That was something the Detective-Sergeant could never take away.

But, it seemed, she was more than happy to hold it against Darcy.

"And here we are again." Darcy kept her tone cheerful as they got seated. She would not let the woman across the table get the best of her.

"Yep." Kaitlin opened her folder, then stared at Darcy for a full thirty seconds. Neither woman blinked.

But Kaitlin looked away first.

"I want to go through what you told me last night one more time. You said that when you left him, Mr. Tufnell was sitting on the couch with his eyes closed."

"Yeah. He was in a good mood. He did seem a little off, though. Like he was tired, or had one drink too many—"

"Something you know from first-hand experience."

Darcy shrugged off the jab. She hadn't had a drink in over five years and was proud of that fact. Her time was too valuable to get into a verbal fight with Kaitlin.

"Or maybe he was just tired. He said he wanted to meditate. He'd put on a high-energy show. It was bound to wear him out. Regardless, he was alive and well when I left that room."

Kaitlin removed an item from a paper evidence bag. It was the Grammy award. A dull, brownish color around its base was unmistakable. And stomach-turning.

"Does this look familiar?" The cop's question was laced with venom.

"Duh, yeah." Darcy pulled up on her phone the photo of her and Derek holding the award. "It's this one right here. So, if my fingerprints are on it, that's why."

"Good try." Kaitlin glanced at a document in the folder. "Our crime scene tech didn't find any fingerprints on it. None. Did you wipe it clean before you whacked Mr. Tufnell with it?"

"No, because I didn't whack him, or anyone for that matter, with that award. Or anything else."

"You and he had a rocky relationship in the past, though. Is that correct?" The cop leaned forward. She stared at Darcy with the focus of a hawk that's spotted a rodent that would soon become dinner.

"Sure, it wasn't the best, but—"

"In fact, you've claimed he sexually assaulted you. When was that?"

Darcy placed her feet on the floor and her hands on her thighs to center her. Then she counted to ten. She blew out a long breath. At that point, she was ready to respond.

"Eight years ago, Pixie Dust and Derek played the same festival. We were finished with our performance when we got word Derek's drummer was sick. Food poisoning, or something like that. Anyway, Derek's rep wanted to know if I'd sit in. A chance to play with a living legend? I said yes in a heartbeat. The performance went fine. When the set was over, he draped himself all over me like a cheap suit and invited me back to his trailer for, as he put it, a nightcap. Then he grabbed my butt, tried to slide his hand up my shirt, and tried to force himself on me. I pushed him away and took off. The end."

"You sure about that?"

"Yes." Darcy fought down a building fire in her belly. "It doesn't matter that there were no witnesses. It's the truth. I mean, why do you think he started trashing me the very next day? I hurt his fragile ego, and he took it out on me by saying I was unreliable as a drummer. That my drinking was out of control. Then, later on, he made a big deal when Pixie Dust fired me that he was right. All he was doing was covering his backside."

"What he said was true, though. Wasn't it? Your drinking was out of control. And you did get fired because of that."

"No." She pointed a finger across the table. It was all Darcy could do to keep from jumping to her feet and shouting at the woman. "I got fired because I got hurt and couldn't play at the level the band needed again."

"But all of that came after the music festival incident, didn't it?" Kaitlin leaned back in her chair and crossed her arms. She smiled, but her icy scare made it clear it wasn't in friendship. "Here's what I think happened. You never forgave Tufnell for what he did to you. Then, like a miracle, a chance to take your revenge fell right into your lap." A knock at the door made Kaitlin stop for a moment, but she recovered with a shake of her head. "You played nice and manipulated everyone so you could be alone with him. Then you let that rage that had built up over the years take over. You grabbed the first thing you could find, the award, and hit him over the head."

Darcy laughed. "Sorry, but that's insane. If you're just going to make stuff up so you can arrest me, I'm done here."

"Not so fast." The knock on the door came again, this time much louder. Kaitlin shouted at the offending person to come in.

"Sorry to bother you, Detective-Sergeant." It was Paul Gerard, the officer who had been first on the scene when Darcy had reported Eddie Maxwell's murder. "Just got the coroner's report."

Kaitlin ripped the papers out of Paul's hand. She stared at the top page, then flipped to the second. She let out a low growl.

"Is this accurate?"

He shrugged. "I don't think they would have sent it if it wasn't."

"Great." She got to her feet and shook her head.

"What's going on? What's it say?" Despite the logical part of her brain telling Darcy to keep her mouth shut, curiosity won out. Any piece of investigation intel she could get was welcome.

"Nothing that concerns you," Kaitlin said.

"Well, since you dragged me down here, I have a feeling it does." Darcy looked from Kaitlin toward Paul. "Come on, if that report proves my innocence, I think I have a right to know."

"I'll be the judge of that." The Detective-Sergeant flipped through the report again. "Okay, fine. You can go. But that doesn't mean you're out of the woods. Make sure Officer Gerard has your contact information in case we need to talk to you again. Get out of here."

Darcy didn't want to give Kaitlin a chance to change her mind, so she left the room at the pace rivaling an Olympic racewalker. Once she was in the hall, she slowed so Paul could come alongside her.

"Any chance I could get you to tell me what's in the report?"

"Why do you want to know?" Despite the unfriendly question, he smiled. It was a warm gesture, not like the frigid one Kaitlin had given Darcy.

"Before you showed up, the She-Devil was about ready to convict me for Derek Tufnell's murder."

"Ah." He gestured for her to follow him outside. "I probably shouldn't share case information with you, but I think this town owes you from last time. The cause of death wasn't blunt force trauma to the head."

Relief coursed through Darcy from her head to her toes. The feeling only lasted for a moment, though, because the information led to another question.

A big one.

"What was the cause of death?"

"The coroner's going to run some more tests to make sure, but it looks like Mr. Tufnell was poisoned."

"How? He was tired, but other than that, he looked fine."

"Toxic levels of antifreeze. Somebody must have put it in whatever he was drinking. We understand he was drinking some kind of flavored water. We're tracking down those bottles to test for traces of antifreeze."

"Yikes. That's pretty cold." An involuntary shiver went through her. Antifreeze sounded like a pretty nasty way to go. "Sorry. Poor choice of words."

"Don't worry about it. You want to know something even weirder?"

"What?" She'd made a promise, to herself and her friends, to figure out who murdered Derek. To do that, she needed information. Especially the kind that came straight from the police.

"According to the coroner, Mr. Tufnell was deceased when he was hit on the head. Which seems to indicate—"

"That the poison made him woozy and he fell and hit his head at the time of death, maybe? Or, what if the person who clocked him is different from the person who poisoned him and didn't know he was already dead?"

Paul nodded. "There's nothing at the crime scene to indicate a fall. So, if we assume what happened lines up with your second scenario, that would mean the poisoner and whoever assaulted him were not aware of each other's activities."

"Great." Darcy rubbed her forehead. "That means there are two murderers running around Marysburg."

She shivered again. One murderer was frightening. Two was downright terrifying. Fear and terror could be conquered, though it was a matter of Darcy being as ruthless in her investigation as the murderers were in criminal acts.

Chapter Five

Darcy was sipping a hot mug of tea on her deck overlooking the convergence of Mary's Creek and the White River when the rustling of leaves on the ground caught her attention.

"Who dares to disturb the ruminations of The Great and Powerful Gaughan?"

"Someone looking for answers in a world full of questions. Mind if I join you?" The visitor was Liam. He was making his usual Sunday Morning visit before he went off to watch English football.

"Pull up a chair."

She waved him onto the deck without turning around. The water's constant flow, mixed with gentle undulations as it made its way over submerged rocks and sticks, calmed her. It served as a reminder that while the world was in a constant state of motion, she could choose to be still. The stillness helped her think. She'd been doing a *lot* of thinking the last day and a half. No answers had come to mind, though,

Liam dropped into a folding camp chair next to Darcy and handed her a white, paper lunch-sized bag.

She took in a deep breath. "Fresh pastries from Jenna's. To what do I owe the pleasure?"

"Figured you had a lot on your mind. A little birdie told me lemon poppyseed muffins go a long way in helping you de-stressify." He took one out and handed the bag back to her. "There are two in there. Knock yourself out."

She glared at him. "Not funny."

"Oh, come on. It was a little bit funny, wasn't it?"

"With the way someone tried to end Derek's life, a tiny bit, at most." She put her nose over the bag's opening and inhaled. "Since you brought these, I forgive you."

With the gusto previously confined to the effort spent behind the drum kit, Darcy tore into the pastries. When she was on the last bite of the first muffin, Liam was barely through a quarter of his.

"Did you even taste that? These are too good to snarf down. You should savor them."

"You sound like my mom. Yes, I solemnly swear by Bob Marley's ghost that I tasted every single last morsel. It was amazing. And I might have skipped dinner last night."

"Tough day yesterday, huh? I stopped by the record store to check out some of the open mic performers. Charlotte said Detective Rosengarten paid you a visit."

"Could have been worse. At least I'm not on her radar as the murderer anymore."

"Did they match fingerprints on the award or get some kind of DNA hit? I mean, it's good you're off the hook, right?"

"Let's see, the answers to those questions, in order, are no, no, and yes." She gave him a beat-by-beat recap of the interview at the police station and how it came to such an abrupt and unexpected conclusion.

"Wow. I was not expecting anything like that. It's going to take a while for me to get my head around that idea that Derek was basically murdered twice."

"Tell me about it." Darcy took a bite of her second muffin and washed it down with some tea. She took the moment of silence to organize her thoughts. Or, try to, to be exact.

"At the end of the day, I think the trophy to the head thing's a distraction. The real murderer is whoever poisoned him. I'm going to have to read up on antifreeze. I mean, how did the poisoner manage to get Derek to drink that stuff? Paul Gerard said they're testing the water bottles he was drinking from. Still, just thinking about it makes me want to barf."

"I'm glad you never found yourself in that position when you were drinking." Liam gave her hand a squeeze. "I've heard stories about people drinking antifreeze since the effects are like drinking alcohol. That's a scary scenario."

"I can't deny there was a time or two when it crossed my mind." She let out a ragged sigh. "I'm lucky I never got that desperate. If not for Eddie, I might have. I feel so bad for the people who end up in a spot like that."

"I never knew that."

"The only person who knew took it to the grave with him. Eddie encouraged me to talk about it, but I never felt strong enough. Maybe someday, though."

They were quiet for a moment. Then Ringo strolled up to them and jumped onto Liam's lap. The microsecond the man started scratching him, the feline began purring loud enough to disturb a nearby blue jay.

"Since the cops let you go, are you going to step aside? I mean, it's not like you need to clear your name anymore." Liam moved from scratching Ringo's back to rubbing the cat's ears.

"On the one hand, I'd like to. I can't, though. Thea asked me to investigate. I couldn't say no. Plus, I'm still honked off about that leak that named me as a suspect."

"Yeah, that was majorly uncool. Any idea who the leaker was?"

"No, but I'd bet my autographed Taylor Hawkins drumsticks that it was Rosengarten. She'd love some payback after I made her look bad back in April. I don't think she'll ever get over me being the one who solved Eddie's murder instead of her."

"Fair enough. Where do you start?"

"Where else? At the beginning." She got to her feet and brushed a few crumbs from her shirt. "Seriously, I think I'll start with the list Hank had me make yesterday."

"Okay." He joined her at the edge of the deck. "Was that before or after Detective R showed up?"

"Detective-Sergeant Rosengarten. She may be like a splinter under my fingernail, but, in her defense, she's got a tough job. We should respect the position, even if we don't have a ton of respect for the person."

Liam barked out a laugh loud enough that it sent Ringo scurrying toward the house. "Wait a minute. A few minutes ago, you were telling me how she was ready to convict you for Tufnell's murder. Now, you're saying we should show her respect? Am I missing something here?"

Darcy chuckled. She had to give her buddy credit. Her change in sentiment about the detective was as abrupt as a time signature change in a jazz tune.

"You're not wrong." She slipped her arm through his. "I did a lot of thinking last night. Last time around, she could dismiss me as a crackpot. And since it was Eddie, the cops were willing to give me some leeway because of how much he meant to me. This time around, things are different, so I'm gonna try the whole 'attracting more bees with honey than vinegar' thing."

"You're a better person than me. If I was in your position, I'd be all like, 'I'll show you, Rosengarten.'"

She gave him a hug. Once again, Liam's knack for saying the right thing came at the exact right time. His comment had been made in jest, but the underlying meaning was one hundred percent serious. The vote of confidence that came with it was worth more than any gold record ever would.

"I figure my time's better spent focusing on the things I can control in the here and now." She glanced at her phone. "Like getting to work. It's just me and the kids today, so I can't be late."

Liam extended his fist. "My friend, you are growing up."

She bumped her knuckles against his. "Correction. Like the Parrothead in Chief Jimmy Buffett said, I may be growing older, but I am not growing up."

* * *

The store was not nearly as busy as the previous day. A weather front had moved in while Darcy got ready for work, bringing steady, cold rain and dropping temperatures. The dreary conditions outdoors had made Peter more determined than ever to make them cheerful indoors.

"We're having a reggae dance party all day, Boss." He dropped the turntable needle on an album by the band Third World. Once the music kicked in, he closed his eyes and began swaying to the languid beat. "That's the ticket, yesi."

She rolled her eyes but took Peter's hand and danced a little number. Izzy recorded the silliness on her phone.

When the song ended, the young man grasped Darcy's wrist and lifted her arm toward the ceiling. "Friends, I give you the Marysburg, Indiana Reggae Dance-Off Champions!"

"I am so going to post this online right now," Izzy said as a middle-aged couple entered the store.

While Peter greeted the customers with wide arms and a wider smile, Darcy joined Izzy to watch the video. When it ended, the young woman looked at her boss. "Can I post it? Please? I'll be sure to tag the store. It'll be good publicity. Promise."

"As long as you credit the songwriters, post away, Iz. Beware, though. I might make you the official Marysburg Music Social Media Manager if it gets a lot of response. Char's already got plenty on her plate."

The younger woman's eyes went wide. "That would so amazing. I mean, since I'm going to Ball State next year, it's not like you'll need to hire someone to replace me."

"Nobody could ever replace you." Darcy gave Izzy a hug. The teenager had been over the moon since she received her acceptance notice from Ball State University.

Darcy had been every bit as thrilled but had encouraged Izzy to temper her excitement until she completed her audition for the School of Music. That wasn't going to happen until after the first of the year. While it gave Izzy plenty of time to rehearse the piece she was going to perform, it also meant that Darcy had plenty of time to remind her how important it was to keep up with her regular rehearsals. On top of everything else, there were scholarship opportunities on the line.

The young woman was too close to the finish line to let herself down now.

Darcy's phone buzzed when the post went live, notifying her that Marysburg Music had been tagged in it. By the time she opened the app, there were already eighteen likes.

"Not too bad for a spur-of-the-moment video, huh?" Izzy bumped her shoulder against Darcy's.

"No argument there." She began scrolling through other posts the store had been tagged in. As she scrolled, the hairs on the back of her neck stood on end. Something about the images from the past few days was bothering her. She couldn't place it, though.

When Peter's customers left the store with a collection of used Leonard Cohen albums in their possession, Darcy called him over.

"Here's a specific case assignment for you. You're both better at the social media game than I am. If we're not busy this afternoon, would you go through the usual sites and see if anything relating to Friday's concert, Derek's death, and the store catches your attention?"

"Sure." Peter gave her a thumbs up. "It's about time you let us help with your investigation."

Darcy had gone to great lengths to keep the kids a long distance from her probe into Eddie's murder. It had been tough enough for her as an adult to deal with the sudden loss of their boss. It hadn't been easy for Izzy and Peter, either. She couldn't bear the thought of adding to that by asking them to help find his murderer.

Now? They were high school seniors. Peter was already eighteen, and Izzy would join turn that age in February. This time next year, they'd both be in college. Adulthood was heading their way fast. Whether that was a good thing wasn't up to Darcy.

What was up to her was how she would deal with the young ones. She'd always treated them with respect, but with a desire to do what she could to protect them from the awfulness that was so often found in the world. She couldn't protect them forever, though.

Nor should she.

It was time to treat them as the responsible adults they were both becoming. At the moment, that included getting their help investigating Derek's murder.

"This is strictly voluntary. If you don't want to do it, that's totally fine. This isn't exactly a happy topic."

"Which makes it even more important that we do our part." Izzy took her phone from her back pocket and gave Peter a friendly punch to his arm. "We're on it."

Darcy's vision became cloudy as her eyes filled with tears. She took a moment to compose herself by dabbing at the corners of her eyes. When she had regained her composure, she exchanged high fives with each of them.

"You two are the best. I'll be in the back working on my suspect board. Let me know if you need anything."

She spent the next half hour researching antifreeze poisoning. While it was a fascinating topic from a science perspective, it was also one that shook Darcy to her core. People turn to drinking antifreeze because the body's response to it is similar to drinking alcohol. Certain chemicals in antifreeze become toxic when the body breaks them down, though, which can lead to injury and death, when consumed in a high enough amount. Given Darcy's past dependence on alcohol, the thought that she could have been among those victims of the awful way to die couldn't be ignored.

All the more reason to find Derek's murderer.

A knock on the office door brought Darcy's research to a halt. It was Izzy. "How's it going?"

Darcy put the pen she'd been using to take notes down. "Making progress. Whoever did this must have administered the antifreeze in smallish doses over a period of time. Like hours. And did it in a way that Derek didn't notice."

The younger woman leaned against the door frame. "Do you know if there were any needle marks on him? You know, maybe someone injected a lethal dose that way?"

"Wow. Lethal dose? Where'd you come up with that? It's pretty dark."

"My mom loves murder mysteries. I like to watch things like *Castle* and *Psych* with her. You can't help picking up a few things along the way."

"Sounds like you should go into criminology if music doesn't work out." They shared a laugh. "Seriously, though, I don't remember needle marks being mentioned. I'll see if I can find out anything."

"Cool." Izzy motioned toward the sales floor. "Anyway, we need you out front. Peter thinks he found something."

"After you." Darcy shot to her feet. For a change, she was happy the store wasn't busy. Just so long it didn't stay that way.

"Check it out, Boss." Peter showed Darcy the screen on his phone. It was a photo of a group standing in front of the theater's marquee. "Someone took this before the show. Look at the dude at the edge of the pic."

The photo showed a profile of the man in question. He didn't look familiar, so Darcy gave a quick nod in acknowledgment.

"Now, check this one out." He showed her another photo taken outside the theater. Again, the same man showed up at the edge of the shot.

This time, most of his face was visible. He had dark hair and appeared to be average height and build. His jacket was dark gray. It didn't feature any logos that Darcy could see.

"Okay, we've got some rando who likes to play photo-bomber." Darcy tapped the image on the screen. "What makes him so interesting?"

Peter and Izzy exchanged a high five. The young man went on to show Darcy eight more photos that included the mystery man. He was always outside the theater and in the background at the edge of every single photograph.

But never the subject.

"It's like this dude wanted to be part of the scene but didn't want people to notice him," Izzy said. "There are a lot of posts from inside during the show, but so far, we haven't found him."

It was some quality detective work. Darcy didn't know what to make of it, though.

"What makes you think he was hanging out all night but didn't actually make it inside for the show?" Darcy scratched her ear. The assumption seemed unlikely, but not unheard of.

"The concert was sold out," Izzy said. "What if he didn't have a ticket and still wanted to be part of the scene? Maybe he was hoping to get an autograph after the show."

"Yeah," Peter said. "Maybe he's some kind of creeper. You gotta admit, the dude looks pretty sketch."

An idea popped into Darcy's head. When she'd been touring with Pixie Dust, she'd come across plenty of overzealous fans. The lead singer and guitarist of the band, Kate Crash, had been forced to get a restraining order issued against one troublesome devotee. The guy was originally from Wichita, Kansas, and had followed the band for nine months. With each passing day, his devotion to Kate became more problematic.

It came to a head one night after a show in San Diego. Somehow, he'd managed to sneak onto the tour bus with the intent of proposing to Kate. The second she climbed on board, he popped out of one of the bunks and got down on one knee in front of Kate. Darcy hit the guy over the head with an empty bottle of bourbon while the bass player, Sandy Goldberg, called the police.

"What if the guy in those pictures is an overly obsessed superfan?" Darcy snapped her fingers. "And even though he couldn't get in, he felt he *had* to be there for Derek's first show on this tour."

Izzy drummed her fingers on the sales counter. "That's a possibility. If you're right, how do we find this guy? It'll be tough Googling him without a name. You know anyone with facial recognition software?"

Darcy knew all too well how easy it was to find someone who'd misbehaved or committed a crime on the Internet. It didn't involve high-end surveillance tech, either. She was also relieved that Izzy didn't seem to possess that knowledge.

At least, not yet.

"Try searching Derek's name with terms like 'restraining order,' 'obsessed fan,' or 'privacy violation.' Things like that. Let me know what you come up with. If you want to use the store's laptop, go ahead, I can handle things out here."

With matching grins, the teens raced to the back room. Despite their enthusiasm, Darcy made a vow that this would be the extent of their involvement. They were still kids, after all.

A bit later, Izzy and Peter returned to the sales floor. Their previous grins were nowhere to be seen.

"No joy, Boss." With slumped shoulders, Peter dropped onto a stool behind the cash register. "We found names of people who were a problem for Derek, but no pictures."

"Sorry." Izzy pushed a piece of paper across the counter toward Darcy. "Here are the names."

She scanned the list. None of the names were familiar. That was okay, though. It was a solid start.

"Great work, you two. Out of the twelve names on this list, seven of them appear to be men. This definitely gives me something to go on."

"How?" the teens asked in unison.

"I'm going to take these names to the biggest Derek Tufnell fan I know of. If anybody knows who stalked him, she does."

Chapter Six

When the workday was finished, Darcy made a beeline to Selena's. Thea was always behind the bar on Sunday nights. With several big-screen TVs showing sports of all varieties, from NBA basketball to IndyCar racing to professional cornhole, and everything in between, it was a good night to serve drinks to a sports-thirsty crowd.

And it made it easy for Darcy to hang out with her buddy for a post-work plate of supreme nachos and a tall glass of ice water.

Normally, it was time for the two friends to catch up on the latest gossip circulating around Marysburg. On this particular evening, once Thea took her order, Darcy got straight to business.

"Before you ask, yes, I'm still investigating Derek's murder. Have the cops gotten ahold of you?"

Thea shook her head. "Why would they?"

"Since she can't pin the murder on me anymore, the Detective-Sergeant will be looking for information wherever she can get it. That includes you and Liam since you were with me after the show."

"You don't think she's going to try to accuse me of murder, do you?" Thea drew herself up to her full six-foot, two-inch height, as if she was ready to take on an entire squad of opponents on the rugby pitch. That, combined with a stony stare she'd taken on, made for an intimidating figure.

"No. You and Liam can alibi each other the whole night. I can vouch for you, too. The same goes for the people who saw you after the show when you stopped for your drinks. What the detective will want from you is information. What did you see? What did you hear? Things like that. You've

47

got nothing to hide, so be honest and don't let her get under your skin."

The rock-hard stare was replaced by Thea's regular grin. "I can do that. Somehow, I get the feeling I shouldn't touch base with your dude to make sure we've got our stories straight. Am I right?"

"That would be a good idea. No need to give Rosengarten a chance to say you've conspired on anything." Darcy took a drink. "And Liam is not 'my dude.' He's my friend. That's it."

"Uh-huh. Just like Frankie's only my friend." Frankie Dugan was Thea's new flame. They'd moved to Marysburg in the summer to take a job at Ball State. They were introduced by a mutual friend after one of Thea's rugby matches. It wasn't quite love at first sight, but she always got a gleam in her eye when mentioning their name.

"If you say so. Anyway, there's a new wrinkle the cops are keeping quiet for now." Darcy filled her in on developments since they'd last spoken.

"I'm glad that gets you off the hook. I can't believe Rosengarten tried to screw you over like that, though."

"What's done is done. I'm not happy about it either, but what that woman says and does won't bring Derek back. What you say and do, however," she pointed a finger at Thea, "might help me identify a suspect."

"What do I gotta do?"

"Help me ID this guy." Darcy showed Thea photos of the man Peter had forwarded to her. While the bartender looked at them, Darcy brought her up to speed on recent developments in the case.

"You think this guy murdered Derek?" She flipped back and forth between two photos. "How? I mean, if he wasn't able to get into the theater, how could he do the poisoning? It's a big jump from stalker to murderer."

"You're not wrong. It's weird he was hanging out all night, though, right? I thought if anyone might know who this guy is and if he caused Derek headaches, it'd be you."

A young person with purple hair seated at the bar a few stools from Darcy signaled to Thea. "Back in a sec. I'll think about it while I take care of this."

While Thea filled a pint glass with a local pilsner for the customer, Darcy looked at the suspect list she'd saved to a note-taking app on her phone. Based on the information she'd read about antifreeze poisoning, the murderer must have had access to Derek for an extended period of time.

Like all day.

Who had that kind of access? That was easy. Everyone traveling with Derek. That meant the band and crew, the manager, the producer. Even theater staff could have done it.

Darcy added the wife, Sophia, to the list. Just because Derek seemed surprised by her appearance, it didn't mean she hadn't been skulking around, plotting against him, while keeping him in the dark.

Thea returned with a slap of her hand on the bar. She whipped out her phone and started ticking away. A moment later, she raised her tattooed arms in triumph. "I know who that guy is. His name's Cameron Jessup. He's from South Bend. A while back he made some claims that Derek stole his song 'Green Eyed Blues' and released it as 'Keep on Knockin.' The guy sued him. Derek denied everything, and the lawsuit got thrown out of court. He wouldn't take no for an answer and started stalking Derek. He claimed that if they could sit down together, he could convince Derek to be reasonable. Cameron's words, not mine."

Darcy scanned an article from *Billboard* magazine Thea showed her. It made Cameron out to be emotionally unbalanced at best and borderline homicidal at worst. Derek had gotten a restraining order against the man twenty years ago.

"Any idea if the court order was still in effect?" Darcy returned the phone to Thea.

"No. But if Jessup is as disturbed as he seems to be, do you think he'd let a piece of paper stop him?"

As one who lived with addiction, Darcy was inclined to give someone with mental illness the benefit of the doubt. At least, at the beginning. The thing she couldn't ignore, though, was that "Keep on Knockin'" had been a huge hit. It had topped the Adult Alternative charts for a month. In terms of crossover appeal, it had been right up there with Santana's smash, "Smooth."

The royalties from a song like that must have been enormous. That didn't include income it generated from being included in a movie soundtrack and on a TV show.

"If he really did write the song, I could totally see how this Cameron dude would have a majorly huge axe to grind." Darcy added the name to her suspect list while Thea attended to another customer.

She also jotted down a few notes next to the man's name. He had motive for days. Anybody could buy antifreeze, so means wasn't a problem. The issue that remained, like a scratch on a record that made the needle skip on a favorite song, was opportunity.

How could Cameron Jessup have murdered Derek?

And if he actually was the murderer, why did he stick around town? To admire the havoc he'd created? It seemed to Darcy all he was likely to get out of remaining in Marysburg was getting himself arrested.

"What do you think, D? Is he our guy?" Thea grabbed a chip from the plate of nachos Darcy had been working through.

"I don't know. Where was his opportunity? Was there an open window somewhere? The back door left open during the load-in? Regardless, now that I've got his name, I'll see what I can find out about him." She took a bite of salsa-laden chip and washed it down with her water. "You were there Friday night. What do you think?"

"We shouldn't count him out."

"We?" Darcy grinned. The use of that particular pronoun warmed her heart. It hadn't been that long ago that the use of "We" in the same sentence as Darcy Gaughan only applied to Ringo.

How times had changed. And for the better.

Thea snorted. "Yeah. It's only a matter of time until that string bean of a detective makes a run at me. Strength in numbers, right?"

They exchanged a fist bump, then Thea drummed her fingers on the bar top. "Anyway, as for suspects other than Cameron, I do remember hearing the drummer, Gwen Crane, ask one of the crew members to pack up her equipment. It didn't go over well."

"Really?" Darcy leaned toward Thea. Her friend had her undivided attention. "Tell me more."

"Well, you were there. It was when we were hanging out and waiting to head back to see Derek. Gwen asked him to pack up her kit and started to walk away. He got all offended and told her that wasn't his job. Then, she got up close to him, said something I couldn't hear, and stomped off.

"Interesting. In the early days of Pixie Dust, I always packed and unpacked my own kit. Later on, though, I had someone do that for me. I'd make adjustments during the sound check, but that was it. With a big name like Derek, I would have thought there'd be enough money in the tour budget for someone to do that for Gwen."

"You think that makes her a suspect?"

Thea stepped away to mix a cocktail and pour two beers for one of the servers. While she was gone, Darcy pondered the question.

With closed eyes, her mind floated back to the previous Friday night. There had been a young woman Darcy didn't recognize staffing a merch table. As she and her friends had neared their seats, two men were stationed behind the soundboard. One of them was the theater's manager, Chris. The other man had dark hair pulled into a man bun. Darcy didn't recognize him, but assumed he was the band's sound tech.

By the time they took their seats, any instrument techs were nowhere to be seen. The performance had gone off without a hitch. Other than Derek's tech helping the star of the show switch guitars from time to time, any other members of the road crew had stayed out of sight until after the encore.

By then, Darcy had been too exhilarated to pay much attention to her surroundings. She'd sat back with a smile, letting the echoes of the evening work their way into her very soul.

Instead of studying the scene and the players. Which, in hindsight, is what she should have been doing. Now, it appeared there were only two techs in total instead of one for each musician. One of them was the sound guy. The other was Derek's guitar tech. Apparently, he didn't take kindly to being asked to help the other musicians.

Thea helped herself to another chip upon her return. The move roused Darcy from her musings.

"Well? Is the drummer our murderer?" Thea scooped some salsa onto another chip and popped it into her mouth.

"First off, as a drummer, I take offense to the idea that any drummer would ever resort to murder. Gotta stand up for my peeps, after all." Darcy took a sip. "Seriously, though, it does raise some questions."

"Like what?"

"Why was the road crew so small? I mean, Derek was a legend. You'd think he'd only tour with full support. That includes a tech for each player."

"How many were there," Thea asked as she poured three beers from a nearby tap.

"Just the two, I think. Was the budget for this part of the tour smaller, which would have meant fewer amenities on the road, like tech support? And if that was the case, did the musicians know that before they signed on?"

"Is that a big deal?"

"Having your own tech makes life a lot easier. They're the unsung heroes of a tour, in my book."

Thea shrugged. "Okay. So, not having one might drive me up a wall. Is it a reason to murder the guy? I mean, now she's out of work. Why not just quit?"

"Good question. Someone of Derek's stature would have had a tour insurance policy. If they did—"

"Ooh." Thea snapped her fingers and pointed them at Darcy. "She wouldn't have to do the tour anymore and might still get paid."

"Slow your roll, girl. One step at a time. I'd like to know what, specifically, she was arguing about. Did she want to get away to do something else? And if so, what?"

"Isn't it obvious? She wanted to slip Derek one last dose of poison before anyone else was allowed backstage."

"That would give her time to do it without being seen by anyone. And maybe even make someone else—"

"Like you."

"Like me, look like the murderer." She got to her feet and extended her fist. "Thea, I believe I have my first two suspects. Gotta go. I have sleuthing to do."

Chapter Seven

Monday morning arrived full of sunshine, but with an unmistakable nip in the air. A sure sign that Mother Nature had her own schedule to keep. No matter how much Darcy wished it wasn't so, the frosty days and frigid nights of Winter weren't far off.

"All the more reason to ride the board today, dude." She placed Ringo's breakfast in front of him. "The kids have their first wind ensemble performance of the year tonight. I promise I'll be home to give you a fancy dinner before I head out again. Deal?"

The cat stopped eating just long enough to look up at her while he swallowed a sliver of grilled chicken. He lifted his head a fraction, as if to let her know that was fine and she was dismissed.

"You're the best, dude. Later, skater." She gave him a few scratches behind his ears, then took off. While waiting for traffic to clear at an intersection, she called the Detective-Sergeant.

"Yes, Ms. Gaughan, what do you want?" The woman let out a long sigh. She was either tired from working long hours since Derek's murder, or she was weary of dealing with Darcy. It was impossible to tell.

"Cameron Jessup. Have you heard of him?" Darcy pushed herself along with full appreciation for how fortunate she was that technology allowed her to ride her board and carry on a conversation at the same time.

"No. Should I have?"

"Yes, because he might be Derek Tufnell's murderer." She told Kaitlin about the conflict between the two men.

Her initial thought had been to keep the information to herself. After talking it over with Ringo when she got home from her visit with Thea, she decided sharing it was the way to go for two reasons. First, she hadn't seen Mr. Jessup since Friday night. If he'd gone back home, the cops could track him down a lot easier than Darcy could. Second, she hoped the Detective-Sergeant would accept the information as a goodwill gesture. Which it was.

"How did you come into this information about Mr. Jessup?"

Not an outright rejection. That was promising.

But it was also asking Darcy to do some fibbing. There was no way she was dragging Thea and the kids into the conversation. Well, sometimes, a girl's gotta do what a girl's gotta do.

"I was scrolling through pictures people posted from the night of the show." She let out a long breath she hoped sounded more dramatic than it really was. "To, you know, process things. This same dude kept showing up in the background of a bunch of pics, regardless of who the poster was."

"Okay. So, how did you manage to connect this mysterious person to a name, a name which just happens to be of someone with a history of legal issues with Mr. Tufnell?"

The force of the question almost threw Darcy off balance. Not a good thing when someone was on a skateboard. Even with a helmet on to protect her noggin, taking a tumble while in motion didn't feel good.

"Something about him seemed off. It's part of my job to know about stuff in the music world. I did some poking around and found about the stolen song claim."

"How do I know you're not making this up?"

Darcy wanted to scream, then grab the woman by the shoulders and shake some sense into her. She was trying to help the investigation, help her community. Yet all this person could do was treat her with an unending barrage of passive-aggressive behavior.

Without the passive part.

She rolled to a stop, then took the phone out of her pocket. "I'm sending you copies of four pics I came across, along with a link to a post I read about

54

the plagiarism dispute. Is that enough for you?"

Kaitlin was silent for a few moments. The silence gave Darcy a chance to get moving again. She was the boss, which to her meant it was doubly important to be at the store on time.

"Tell you what." The cop's words seemed to be forced out of her, like Darcy's were back when her tour manager made her reveal where she'd hidden bottles of booze. "We'll take this information under advisement. Thank you for your support of the Marysburg Police Department."

The connection ended.

"Well, frac." A few strong strokes of her leg, born of frustration-induced adrenaline, propelled Darcy along at a pace that had her shooting past runners like they were standing still. At some point, attempts to build bridges with the Detective-Sergeant became nothing more than exercises in madness.

She was getting close to that point.

By the time Charlotte arrived at the record store, Darcy had turned the frustration into fuel.

"Whoa. This place is spotless." She took a look at her reflection in the sales counter glass. "Did you get here early to give it a super scrub?"

"Had some extra energy to burn this morning." Darcy related her conversation with Kaitlin. "I want her to see me as being part of the solution. That I don't hold dragging me down to the police station the other day against her. I guess I was being stupid."

"You weren't being stupid." Charlotte took a dust cloth out of Darcy's hands. "You were trying to take the high road."

"Yeah. And look where it got me."

"You know something, Darc? Self-pity doesn't look good on you." She put her hand up to stop any retorts. "'You can't control what other people do. You can only control what you do.' A woman who I thought was pretty smart told me that a few years ago. It's good advice. Maybe you should follow it."

Darcy stared at the concrete floor while she digested Charlotte's stern but loving reprimand. Having her own words come back to haunt her was always tough. She let out a long breath.

"You're right." She raised her head until her gaze met Char's. "I tried to do a good thing. What Rosengarten chooses to do with the information is out of my control. What I can control is how I conduct my investigation."

"That's more like it." Charlotte brushed a lock of purple-tinted hair out of her eyes. "Now go back there and work on your suspect board. And I will brew a pot of coffee since there's no tidying up to do."

It was like a weight of a thousand record albums had been lifted from Darcy's shoulders. Charlotte's pep talk had been just what the doctor had ordered. She would cooperate with the police whenever she could. She would not let Detective-Sergeant Kaitlin Rosengarten derail her efforts to find justice for Derek.

She stopped at the entrance to her office when a thought came to her. Paul Gerard had given her the poisoning information without any fuss. He seemed willing to work with her despite his colleague's reluctance. Maybe she was reading too much into that exchange. On the other hand, maybe he could become her go-to source at the police station.

The upbeat rapping of Lizzo came over the store's stereo system. It got Darcy moving. There was work to be done.

Before she could turn her attention to the suspect board, Darcy had to channel her inner Elvis and take care of business. Of the record store. She spent thirty minutes ordering new merch. Despite the somber mood, sales had been brisk Saturday. She shrugged. At least one good thing had come out of that grief-filled day.

Next, she took a few minutes to make sure the store's social media posts were scheduled to her satisfaction. Char had recently taken over the task from Darcy. At the time, she claimed Darcy's social media game rated a C minus.

In the five weeks since the task changed hands, visits to the store's website had increased by twenty percent, with a corresponding increase in online sales. Engagement with the store's social media posts had gone up, too. The results spoke for themselves.

Still, Darcy liked to know what content had been scheduled. She told everyone it was to check for the random typo. To Ringo, she said it was to make sure nothing got posted that could come back to bite the store in the backside. Charlotte would never do anything to hurt the store. There was no doubt about that. Even an innocent mistake could cause problems.

And Darcy was the one who was ultimately responsible.

A little while later, Charlotte knocked and opened the door. "We've got a customer who asked to speak only to you."

"Ugh. Not the best timing." Darcy's mentor Eddie Maxwell had cultivated relationships with a large number of customers who preferred to deal with only him. Since his sudden passing, she'd worked hard to develop relationships with those same folks. "Who is it?"

"Heather Ewing."

"Really." Darcy froze. It took her a moment to run through the possible scenarios involved with greeting Eddie's neighbor and long-term friend of the record store, then she plastered on a smile. "This could get interesting. Let's see what she wants."

"You sure about this? I can have Nine-One-One pulled up on my phone. Just to be on the safe side."

"Let's hit pause on that and give her the benefit of the doubt." She put her arm around Charlotte. "It wasn't that long ago that my situation wasn't all that different from what she's in now."

The women found the visitor flipping through albums in the world music section. She already had a copy of Paul Simon's *Graceland* under one arm.

Char veered off toward the cash register while Darcy cleared her throat. She came to a stop ten feet away from the woman. It was the first time Darcy had seen her in months.

"It's been a minute, Heather. How can I help you?"

The woman placed her purse and the album on top of the stack of records she'd been looking at. She looked Darcy in the eye, bit her lip, and wiped a tear from her cheek.

"Thank you for seeing me. I never meant for things...." Another tear ran down the side of her face.

Darcy took Heather in her arms and held her close. Kindness and compassion were two things that never went out of style. As the woman sobbed, Darcy tightened her hold. She knew all too well how the pain people carried could eat them up from the inside until it destroyed them.

That had almost been Darcy.

"I know you didn't." She caught Charlotte's eye, then nodded toward the office and guided the woman there, so she could grieve in relative privacy.

Darcy hovered nearby until Heather's tears came to an end. One of the many valuable lessons she learned in rehab was that it was healthy to have all kinds of emotions. People weren't robots. Some days were tough, so it was one hundred percent normal to be sad or angry.

It was when people tried to cover up, or ignore, the negative emotions that they were headed for trouble. The best thing Darcy could do for Heather was let the woman express her grief without judgment.

Suck it up, Buttercup, was not part of Darcy's vocabulary.

She shook her head as she handed Heather another tissue. Someone coming to her for support. My, how had times changed.

"Char makes an amazing cup of coffee. Can I get you one?"

Heather nodded. "Two sugars, please."

When she returned, she sat behind her desk. "What's up, Heather? I have a feeling you're not here for a music recommendation."

"Not just that, no." She chuckled and pointed at the blanket-covered whiteboard. "I take it you're at it again? Fighting crime and all that?"

The murder of Darcy's boss Eddie Maxwell and the subsequent capture of his murderer had dealt a double blow to Heather. She'd even gone as far as helping Darcy investigate the matter without realizing how much danger she herself had been in.

"I am. My nemesis, the good Detective-Sergeant, wanted to set me up as the murderer. I won't put up with that."

"Here we go, again. Just like six months ago."

Darcy held her tongue. The circumstances this time around were way different than those involving Eddie's murder. Well, except for the fact that Kaitlin still had a chip on her shoulder when it came to Darcy.

"I could use the Detective-Sergeant's attitude toward me as motivation. I'm not doing that, though. Somebody murdered Derek. He started his tour here as a gesture to me. I believe he was sincere in his effort to make amends for his past behavior. The way for me to pay that back is to do everything I can to make sure the murderer, the right one, sees justice."

Heather smiled. "You're a remarkable woman, Darcy. You know that?"

"Thank you. That's kind of you to say. I'm a total work in progress, though. One day, maybe."

"I want to help you. With the investigation. I have a lot I want to make up for. Please?"

"Of course." Darcy reached across the desk and took the woman's hand in hers and gave it a reassuring squeeze. The belief the people in Marysburg had in her was humbling beyond words. Maybe someday she'd write a song about it. That's the way she used to deal with her feelings.

Couldn't hurt to try. After Derek's murderer was put away.

"Thank you." Heather practically leapt to her feet. "What's my first assignment?"

Since the woman's desire to help was sincere, Darcy would put her to work.

"Spend as much time out in public. You know, around people. Keep your eyes and ears open for anything about Derek. No detail's too small or insignificant."

"How will that help?"

"Right now, my main suspects are all out-of-towners. People who knew Derek. I want you to see if anyone from here in town had a grudge against him."

Heather had spent enough years working in the community that she knew a lot of people. She was also seen as an innocent victim in all the unfortunate events surrounding Eddie's murder. Folks wouldn't be inclined to hold their tongues in her presence.

That was the hope.

"I'll let you know what I find out." As she left the office, she seemed to be walking a little taller.

Darcy understood the need for redemption. Whether it was a real need or only a perceived one. And the feeling of empowerment when someone showed belief in you. It was truly all about being part of the solution.

That evening, Darcy and Charlotte closed the record store early. Initially, Char had been reluctant, but gave in when the boss refused to relent.

"Awfully last minute, Darc." Char shrugged as she taped a closed-early sign to the door.

"Things happen, girlfriend. I've posted the closing on social. I'll apologize if anyone gets their nose out of joint. The kids are seniors. We won't get to see them perform many more times."

"Oh, don't you dare play the guilt card on me."

"Why not? You've used it on me more times than Kiss has gone on farewell tours."

They laughed as Darcy locked up for the night. Kiss was one of the store's steady sellers. Darcy appreciated how much the legendary glam band contributed to the bottom line. Still, she could have sworn they'd played five farewell tours. That seemed excessive.

On the walk to the high school, they talked about who they'd want to see most come out of retirement to perform a show.

"That's easy. Go-Go's all the way. I'd donate a kidney to see Gina Schock perform *We Got the Beat* with the rest of the band." Darcy performed an air drum roll as she sang the song's refrain.

"Not bad. I'd love to see Chuck Mangione. Those King of the Hill episodes he was on were golden. Man, the second I hear one of his songs, my mood always improves."

"Your mood should improve tonight, then. Peter told me the wind ensemble is performing pieces from Hollywood blockbusters."

"Cool. Any idea if he or Izzy are performing solos?" Charlotte picked up the pace. Evidently, now that her reservations about closing early were dealt with, she was ready to enjoy an evening of music performed by Marysburg High School's finest musicians.

"Not this time around. Peter promised me they'd be in the spotlight during their December holiday concert, though."

They reached their seats in Marysburg High's auditorium as the lights went down. Despite the fact that Darcy's two employees didn't get to bask in the spotlight, it was a fantastic show. The ensemble hit all the big names—James

Horner, John Williams, Randy Newman, and more.

The young musicians played flawlessly. The music enveloped Darcy like a warm blanket on a chilly October night. As she relaxed, her mind wandered. After a while, it arrived at the case. She didn't fight it. Instead, she let the rhythms the high schoolers produced propel her thoughts in the direction they wanted to go. The unfocused musings let her look at the facts she had so far from a variety of perspectives.

And like a well-known tune, one familiar theme kept returning to her. Regardless of how she studied it, on the surface, Cameron Jessup was a logical murder suspect. Revenge was a strong motivator, after all. Except for one issue that wouldn't go away.

Now that Derek was dead, Cameron would never get the apology he claimed many times he was owed. Along with songwriting credit and the royalties that came with it, of course.

Why kill the potential cash cow?

By the time the performers rose from their seats to enjoy a hearty round of applause from the audience, Darcy finally landed on the basis of a theory she liked.

The murder was premeditated. Other than that, the investigation was still in its early stages. It was way too early for her to home in on a single suspect. She'd leave that to Kaitlin and her snap judgments.

For Darcy, it meant the investigation continued. And she knew exactly who she needed to talk to next. From the frying pan and into the fire. Hopefully, she wouldn't end up getting burned.

Chapter Eight

Derek's band and crew were staying at the Marysburg House. The three-story Victorian mansion was built in 1887 by a wealthy railroad baron by the name of Shoemaker. It remained in his family until 1980, when his youngest granddaughter passed away without a will. The house sat vacant for years until Todd Meadows' father bought it and turned it into a bed & breakfast.

Since then, the structure stood as a testament to the finest of nineteenth century grandeur combined with twenty-first century convenience. The complimentary wi-fi was as fast and reliable as the coffee was hot and tasty. There were eight guest suites. One was on the main floor, five on the second floor and two on the third floor. Each of them had a private bathroom that came with the thickest and most absorbent towels in the county.

When news about Derek's murder got out, the Marysburg House worked with the police to make sure the band and crew had a place to stay for a few days.

For Darcy, she only had to visit one place to get answers. Convenience like that was welcome any day.

She found the band's rhythm guitarist and bass player, Drew Easton, on the front porch. He was looking at something on a laptop while he sipped from a ceramic mug emblazoned with the bed & breakfast's logo.

"Hey, Drew. Mind if I join you?" She took a seat in the rocking chair next to him without waiting for a response.

He brushed his curly brown hair from hie eyes and nodded. "Been a while, Darcy. Nice little town you've got here."

"Thanks. I'm really sorry about all of this. Heck of a way to find yourself with down time. How are you doing?"

"You know how it is." He put his computer on a little table next to him. "You spend so much time rehearsing and getting to know everyone and then, boom, it all blows up in a puff of smoke."

Drew was an in-demand touring musician. In his two decades on the road, he'd performed with dozens of rock and blues stars all over the world. Whenever Derek went out on tour, Drew was there, including that fateful festival gig Darcy sat in on that led to her falling out with Derek.

"Yeah, what a shame. He was in such a good mood when we talked after the show." When Drew didn't respond, she decided to apply some pressure. "You seem to be taking things in stride."

"What are you going to do?" He took a drink of his coffee. "This redemption tour thing of his was a load of bull. I'm glad he apologized to you, but he hadn't exactly turned over a new leaf like a lot of people thought."

"What do you mean?"

"You saw him stumbling around that night. He looked like someone who'd had too much to drink. And the other thing? Let's just say I won't be surprised if it was his wife or Gwen who did him in."

"The other thing? Are you saying he was harassing women again?"

"Again? More like still." Drew leaned forward and put his elbows on his thighs. "Don't get me wrong. I worked with Derek for a long time. Back in the day, we'd laugh or shrug off his misbehavior. While I can't speak for anyone else, for me, the wild and crazy rock and roll lifestyle on the road is a thing of the past. It should stay there. I've got a husband and two kids back home. I video chat with them every day. A lot of stuff that used to be okay back then, the drugs, the booze, the groupies, that's not cool nowadays."

Darcy's mind raced as a myriad of emotions worked their way through her. Shock at the revelation Derek hadn't stopped his womanizing. Anger that he lied about it. Disappointment that she fell for his ruse hook, line, and sinker.

There would be time for self-reflection later. At the moment, her resolve to catch the murderer grew stronger. She wanted the truth to come out, now more than ever.

"You mentioned Gwen and his wife. Why?"

"Sophia, God love her, put up with a lot. She really loved Derek, despite all the bad stuff he did behind her back. She's the one who stuck by his side all those years before he finally went into rehab. The fact that she showed up here, out of the blue, tells me one thing. She found out about his cheating and was going to have it out with him once and for all."

"Do you think she was angry enough to murder him? After all they'd been through?"

"All I know is that when he got sober, he promised Sophia he'd never cheat on her again."

Darcy did a little drum roll with her right hand on her thigh. She didn't know much about Derek's widow. The woman had kept a low profile throughout his career, first raising their two daughters in a tony suburb of Boston, then getting involved in a number of charitable causes when the kids were grown. By a number of accounts, she chose to put up with her husband's misbehavior in exchange for a life of financial security for herself and the children.

Maybe she'd decided the terms of that deal had ended and had taken things into her own hands.

"Well, he won't be doing that now, that's for sure." She chuckled. "Sorry. That was awful of me."

"No apology needed. I get it. I mean, look at me. I'm stuck in this little town in the middle of Flyover Country with no idea when this nightmare's going to end. I don't know whether to laugh or cry."

Darcy ignored the dig at her hometown. Sure, Marysburg was no Miami or Seattle, but it was her home. And she loved it.

"You also mentioned Gwen. Why is that?" She had a good idea, but she wasn't going to put words in anyone's mouth.

"Derek was harassing her. At first, it was jokes he'd make about her being too pretty for his own good. They seemed harmless enough. Even Gwen laughed at the beginning. As rehearsals went on, he started to get more forward with her. Since I was the one who recommended her to Derek, I told him if he didn't stop it and apologize, I'd tell Sophia."

"Bringing in the big bass drum. How'd that go over?"

"Better than I expected, actually. He promised he'd do better. I believed him. At the end, I think he was just telling me what I wanted to hear."

"Why's that?"

"The last day of rehearsal, Derek put together a little celebration. A few drinks, some cake. Not a big deal, but it was nice. Leave people in a good mood before rolling out, you know? When it was over, I found a quiet corner and had my call with the family. After I finished saying goodbye to my kids, I heard raised voices, like people arguing."

"Did you recognize the voices?"

"They were behind closed doors, but there was no mistake. It was Derek and Gwen. They weren't having a pleasant conversation."

"What did you hear?"

"A lot of accusations back and forth. At the end, she said, 'If you won't come clean, I will.' I heard footsteps, so I got out of there before they could catch me listening in."

"Wow." That was all Darcy could come up. She'd set out for the bed & breakfast, hoping to find a crumb or two to follow. Now, she had two serious suspects.

"Yeah. Why all the questions? You're not a part-time cop when you're not at your record store, are you?"

"No, I'm not." She rubbed her hands together. "I was so excited that Derek chose to kick off the tour here because he wanted to see me. And now he's dead. In my hometown. How awful is that? I can't sit by and do nothing."

"So, you're playing a lady version of Benoit Blanc?"

Darcy barked out a laugh. There were worse things than being compared to the Daniel Craig character from the *Knives Out* movies. The break in conversation gave her a chance to regroup. She didn't want Drew to become defensive. That might end up with him keeping things from her.

Which wouldn't be good.

"Good one." She shook her head. "You said it yourself. This is a small

65

town. I'm the only one around who's lived the life of a touring musician. I wanted to see how everyone was doing. And I wanted to give y'all someone to commiserate with who gets what life on the road is like. Does that make sense?"

He looked at his coffee mug. After a while, he took a drink.

"I guess I can see that. Gotta admit, it's good to have someone to talk to who isn't from the cops or the band."

"In that case, tell me about your kids. I remember a quote from you back in the day where you said you were a lifelong bachelor. What happened?"

Drew laughed this time. "Don't hold that quote against me. Swear to God, that's what I thought at the time. Then, I met a physical therapist when I was rehabbing my shoulder after a bicycling injury. When my treatment was done, I asked him out. The rest is history."

They talked about family for a while, then his phone's ringtone went off.

"I need to get this. It's my manager."

She mouthed a thank you as she got to her feet. Pleased with the information she'd obtained, Darcy wandered inside. Next on her set list was a chat with Gwen.

The woman was on the backyard patio, playing an electronic drum kit. With a set of Beats headphones in use, the only sound she was making was the rhythmic tapping of the drumsticks on the drum pads. It was an interesting sight. Both arms and legs were moving, yet virtually no sound was being created.

Technology was pretty amazing at times.

Taking care not to surprise her fellow drummer, Darcy took a wide, circular path until she was in Gwen's line of sight. Then she waved.

"What's up, Darcy?" Gwen tossed a drumstick to her while she pulled another one from a pouch at her feet without missing a beat. "Wanna jam?"

Darcy twirled the wooden stick through her fingers. It was thinner than the ones she used. Not a surprise, given how hard she played back in the day.

Gwen unplugged her headphones. The Ramones' "I Wanna Be Sedated" came through a small set of speakers. The pull of playing along with the Godfathers of Punk couldn't be denied. Darcy went to Gwen's side, grabbed another stick, and spent the next fifteen minutes banging away to a collection of classic punk anthems.

When her elbow began to ache, Darcy had called it quits.

"Does it ever make you mad?" Gwen pointed at Darcy's elbow. "Not being able to play like you used to?"

She shrugged and returned the sticks to their holder. "A few people have reached out to me, said they could teach me a new way to drum. That I could play without putting so much stress on the elbow. I don't want to do that, though. I had fun playing that way. I've made my peace with where I am."

"That's cool." Gwen sighed as she pulled her shoulder-length blond hair into a ponytail. "Right now, being a retired drummer doesn't sound too bad."

"I'm so sorry. I can't imagine how hard this has been on you."

"Thanks. The cops have been pretty chill. When they asked us all to stick around for a few days, I was like, well, my calendar's clear right now."

"You must be anxious to put all of this in your rearview mirror."

"You're not wrong. I was counting on this tour to open some doors for me. You remember how hard it is for a woman in this business, right? Especially a drummer?"

"I do. That's part of the reason I started Pixie Dust."

"You were one of my inspirations. Me and some friends saw you when we were in high school. I won't listen to any Dust music from after you left the band."

Darcy smiled. It had taken a long time, but she was now at the point where she held no ill will toward the current members of Pixie Dust. She'd even forgiven their manager, who lied to her about having her back up until the day they kicked her out of the band.

"Their new music's not bad. Yvonne Schmidt's a good drummer. Nice person, too. I'd be happy to put you in touch with her if you want."

Gwen's eyes went wide. "You'd really do that?"

"Why not? A rising tide lifts all boats, and that kind of thing. Give me your digits." Darcy had spoken many kind words about Yvonne when she was announced as Pixie Dust's new drummer. It wasn't her replacement's fault she'd gotten hurt and that her drinking was out of control.

Besides, the periodic royalty payments she got from the band helped pay the bills. At the end of the day, there was no reason not to be magnanimous.

She typed out an introductory text. The response was immediate. And positive.

"Thanks so much. If there's anything I can do to return the favor, please let me know."

"Since you mentioned it, I was wondering if I could talk to you about Derek. I understand you were the one who found him. That must have been horrible."

Hitting Gwen with the question right after helping might have been a manipulative move. On the other hand, Darcy needed the information in her counterpart's possession.

"It was." A shiver went through her. "I'd finished packing up my kit and was going to have a word with him. The door was open a bit, so when he didn't respond to my knock, I went in. And there he was. Not moving or anything."

Darcy told her about finding Eddie, leaving the worst parts out. At the same time, she made a mental note to follow up about the drum kit. Thea had seen something quite different from what Gwen had just told her.

"It's hard. Especially when there are things left unsaid. What were you going to talk to him about?"

"I don't even remember. It's pointless now."

"Don't be so sure about that. Derek might have been nice to me, but I've heard some stories that he was up to his old tricks again." That wasn't one hundred percent the truth, but close enough for Darcy to sleep well. "Was he pressuring you to do anything against your will?"

Gwen crossed her arms and leaned back. "Hold on a minute. What are you saying?"

The goodwill Darcy had manufactured was headed out the door. She needed to pull the conversation back in the direction she wanted before Gwen shut her down.

"That Derek may have been a legendary musician, but he was a legendary sexual predator, too. If he said anything inappropriate or tried to force you into something, you're not alone. It's okay to speak out. Don't carry that alone."

Gwen twirled a drumstick through her fingers and stared at something in the distance. Her hesitance told Darcy enough. The question now was whether Derek had pressured Gwen enough that it led to his murder.

"Okay, yes. At first, things were fine. I was making music with a living legend, right? And getting paid for it. Then he started getting a little too friendly. I mean, the guy was old enough to be my grandpa. I told him to back off. He did."

A tear ran down her cheek as she sucked in a long breath.

"When we got into town here, Derek cornered me on the tour bus after everyone else got off. Asked if he could have a word alone with me. We'd had a fight the last day of rehearsal and hadn't spoken since."

"I'm so sorry." Darcy gave Gwen a reassuring squeeze.

"That's okay." She sniffed. "Feels good to get this off my chest. Anyway, I knew what Derek had done in the past. I told him I wasn't going to let him get away with it anymore. He needed to do the right thing."

"Did he threaten you in any way? Like, to fire you and then make sure you never got a drumming gig again?"

"No. Instead, he begged me to forgive him. That he was going to make things right. He just needed a few days. I pushed him to the side and got off the bus. We didn't speak the rest of the day. The show went well. I thought I'd try to mend some fences with him. You know, figure out how we could work together."

"And that's when you found him."

"Yep. The last thing I said to him was 'Do what's right for once.' I never got to apologize for that."

Darcy let it go at that. She'd put Gwen through enough already. While she felt for the young drummer, she couldn't ignore one fact that was as large as a bass drum.

She hadn't told the truth about packing up her equipment. Why would she do that unless she had something to hide?

Chapter Nine

After all the information she gathered from Drew and Gwen, Darcy was ready for some time to think. She didn't have her thoughts organized enough to visit Selena's and hash things out with Thea. Instead, a place where she could make notes on her phone undisturbed was the ticket.

That meant a trip to the Big Bean, Marysburg's premier coffee house. It was Marysburg's only coffee house. That didn't change the fact that if it had competition, it would come out on top.

She took a spot near the front picture window so she could watch the world go by while she pondered. The steam from her green tea curled toward the ceiling as the aroma filled her with happy thoughts. While she sipped the hot drink, she worked on her notes.

Drew wasn't a strong suspect. He simply didn't have much of a motive. Still, he didn't seem broken up about Derek's passing, either. Was his comment about Gwen an attempt to throw Darcy off his scent?

After the show, she'd crossed paths with Hambone backstage, but Drew had been nowhere to be seen. At this stage of the investigation, anything was possible.

Then there was Gwen. That was some blockbuster information she'd shared. Darcy wanted to believe the woman. The spirits above knew how tough it had been being the subject of Derek's despicable behavior, and that was only a single incident.

The problem that couldn't be ignored, though? The woman had lied about where she was at the time of Derek's murder. Why was that?

70

She took a sip and watched a pair of birds flit from one store awning across the street to another and then back again. Her avian distraction ended when Vanessa Perez, the band's tour manager, entered the shop.

A flame of inspiration ignited and sent Darcy to the cashier.

"Hey, Lenny. I've got this woman's order." She handed her credit card to the young man behind the register.

Vanessa looked up, digging in her purse. She raised her eyebrows when she recognized her benefactor.

"Thank you, Darcy. That's very kind of you."

"No big. I figure you and everyone else with the band could use as much kindness as you can get."

"It's been a nightmare." The woman took her drink order to a counter and stirred three packs of natural sweetener into it. "I feel like I've spent every waking moment since Friday night either on phone calls or emails. Venues, vendors, suppliers—you name it. What an absolute disaster."

Darcy nodded toward her spot. "Care for some company? People around here tell me I've become a pretty good listener."

Vanessa laughed, which made her silver, dangly earrings sway back and forth. She dropped her purse on the table and eased onto the stool across from Darcy.

"I needed that laugh, thanks." She put her hands up. "That doesn't mean you weren't a good listener in your Pixie Dust days. You just—"

"Thought I had all the answers and was going to use them to conquer the world."

"Your words, not mine." She placed her phone on the table. Screen down. "I could use some down time. I don't think I've had a second to reflect on what's happened. I mean, it's such an absolute shame. Derek hadn't sounded this good in years. I had so many plans."

"Like what?"

"This tour of small venues was just the beginning. After the first of the year, we were going to move to larger theaters, take a month off to rest, and hit amphitheaters and festivals during the summer. It was all coming together."

Darcy offered her condolences. The double whammy of losing her client and her plans for the next year had to be overwhelming. The mention of her plans opened a door for a few questions, though.

"I know the tour was just getting started, but do you know if there were arrangements to keep the band together through the whole run you mentioned?"

"Yes. Through the end of the year, at least. Why do you ask?"

"I got the sense there was some tension among the band. Like people where already not getting along." That was putting it mildly.

Vanessa flicked her wrist like she was batting away a gnat. "Of course, tension was high. It was the start of the tour. People were still getting to know each other. In a few weeks, it was going to be smooth sailing."

"Really?" The word was out before Darcy realized it. She grimaced. It wasn't the term that had her cheeks getting hot. It was her disbelieving tone. "Sorry about that. I guess I'm surprised that you had so much confidence in everyone so early in the process."

"Call me an optimist, but I had high hopes for this group." She scratched an earlobe. "I guess I was overly optimistic."

"Why do you say that?" Now they were in the groove Darcy wanted to follow.

"Isn't it obvious?" She leaned toward Darcy. "I probably shouldn't tell you, but it turns out the cause of Derek's death wasn't a blow to the head. He was poisoned."

"Oh, wow. How awful." Darcy covered her mouth with her hand to drive home her fake surprise. Paul had divulged the information to her in confidence. It still hadn't been made public. She wasn't going to betray him. "Do you know if the police have any leads?"

"If they do, they're not saying. Probably so they don't get caught jumping the gun like they did with you."

"Yeah, well, let's just say that the detective and I share a history. That doesn't matter now. Has she talked to you?"

"I think she's talked to everyone with the tour by now. She's keeping tight-lipped about the investigation."

"I can imagine. Did she mention what kind of poison was used?"

Darcy had done her research on antifreeze poisoning. It would have taken hours for the toxin to build up to a level that became lethal. That meant Derek must have started ingesting the poison around the time the group arrived in town. Establishing where suspects were at the time of arrival was every bit as important as nailing down where they were at the time of death. In this case, timing was proving to be everything.

"No. And there I was, the tour manager, supervising the load out, when Derek needed me the most. It drives me crazy to think I was only a few feet away when he died. If only I could have been there...."

"That kind of thinking leads to madness. The most important thing you can do now is to keep giving the police your full cooperation. Then take it one hour, one day, at a time. Believe me, I know."

"Yeah. I heard about your crime-fighting exploits this past Spring. That's amazing. Did you ever get scared?"

"I was scared out of my wits for days. Focusing on two things kept me going. Keeping the record store open and figuring out who killed Eddie. Maybe you could try something like that. Find one or two things you can concentrate on."

"I'll try that. Thanks."

"Here's my business card. However long you're here, if you need something, call or come visit the store."

They chatted for a few more minutes, then Vanessa had to get going. She had a call with an insurance adjuster. Darcy gave her a hug. That was one call she was glad she didn't have to be a part of.

Once she was alone again, she went back to the notes on her phone. The conversation with Vanessa helped illuminate one point.

The likelihood that Cameron Jessup was the murderer had diminished. Did he whack Derek over the head? That was still totally in the realm of possibility. But administering him poison over the course of hours? That sounded like an inside job.

That term again—an inside job.

Which meant Darcy needed to talk to more people in Derek's organization.

Like Brian McGuinness, the man who had just entered the coffee shop. Thank goodness for small favors. Like the fact that the coffee house was only two blocks from the Marysburg House.

As she got up, she made a mental note to come here when she was in the mood to people-watch. There was a constant flow of foot traffic.

"I've got this guy's order, too, Lenny. And another for me." Darcy reintroduced herself to Brian.

"Right, from the other night." He shook her hand. "Vanessa suggested I come here. I've been craving a good cappuccino. What an unexpected pleasure seeing you again."

"Yeah, imagine that. How are you holding up?"

"It's been tough. One minute, we were all looking forward to great things. The next, he was gone. Given all he'd been through, we started a running joke that the only musician he wouldn't outlive was Keith Richards."

Darcy laughed. "Yeah, Keith is indestructible. You and Derek worked together for a long time, didn't you?" She directed him to her "interview" table.

"For thirty-five years."

"It was nice of you to come to town for the show. That's unusual for a producer to join an artist on tour, isn't it?" Darcy knew the answer but was in full detective mode. She wanted to hear it from him.

"Yeah." He took a sip, closed his eyes, and practically melted in his chair. "That is one fine drink. To be honest, I didn't expect to find something this good in a town like this."

Darcy let the insult pass. Sure, Marysburg was small, but it had a lot of things going for it. Like a wonderful, locally owned coffee shop. If one more member of Derek's group insulted it, though, she would be done holding her tongue.

"At least you got to see his final performance. It was a good one. It may have been a small venue, but he went out on top."

"That he did. Which makes his death all the more painful. You see, I wasn't certain Derek was as on form as he was claiming. He wanted to record a live album and make a documentary of his comeback tour. I wanted to see for myself before I committed to anything."

"Ugh." Darcy dropped her chin to her chest. "Talk about a punch to the gut. At least you got to see that he was telling the truth."

"Yes. It was an excellent show. It's been gratifying to see the outpouring of love for Derek. At least, with this one final show, people will remember him for all the right reasons."

Darcy's radar went on alert. What exactly did he mean by all the right reasons? Was a clue in her midst? She didn't feel like tiptoeing around this possibility and missing out.

"The right reasons?"

"Onstage, as the musical genius he was. Yes, he made a lot of poor choices in his life and hurt a lot of people. But music was his true legacy. Think about it. Elvis, Michael Jackson, George Michael. All those artists were geniuses who fought their demons. At the end of the day, people remember them for their music. And now, it'll be the same with Derek Tufnell."

Darcy chewed on her lip as she debated how to respond. Derek's problem with alcohol abuse wasn't demons. It was a medical condition for which he eventually sought treatment. As someone who went through rehab to get sober, Darcy could tip her drumstick to the deceased for his efforts in that arena.

His sexual predator activities were another matter. From Darcy's perspective, those were decisions he made of his own free will. He chose to take advantage of his position of power as a famous white male to abuse women, including his wife.

Then, to claim that he'd changed and was sincere in his efforts to make amends and have it turn out to be a big sham? Well, Darcy believed in forgiveness. But that belief only went so far.

And Derek had crossed that line.

"I've heard he was harassing women again. Any idea if that's true? Because if it's true, then that makes it tough to not speak ill of the dead. Know what I mean?"

Brian sat up straight and looked Darcy in the eye. The seconds ticked by on the digital clock above the shop's cash register. Eventually, he took a drink. When he put his cup down, he cleared his throat.

"I do. And given your history with him, I understand your concern. I want to assure you I knew nothing about any inappropriate behavior. Assuming he engaged in any, that is. Which I don't have any reason to believe he did."

"Good to know." Darcy decided to let it go.

For now.

It wasn't out of the realm of possibility that Brian was telling the truth. After all, he was Derek's producer. He wouldn't be involved with the intimate details of the lead up to the tour. That was Vanessa's responsibility.

"Did anyone record the show?" Darcy asked. Some touring acts, like O.A.R., recorded all their shows and made the recordings available to purchase. Others, including such disparate acts as Disturbed and The Flaming Lips, recorded performances at special venues, like Red Rocks Amphitheatre.

"I haven't thought to ask." His eyes lit up as he got to his feet. "What an opportunity if it was, though. I'll look into it right now. Thanks."

He practically sprinted out the door, talking a mile a minute on his phone. Maybe Darcy was being over-sensitive, but Brian's sudden excitement left a bitter taste in her mouth. Sure, Derek's group could use any silver linings they could get. But a recording of Derek's final performance wasn't at risk of going bad, like a banana left out in the sun too long. All Brian needed to do was talk to the sound tech. It was probably stored on a cloud-based server. Safe and sound.

What if that was Brian's endgame, though? A posthumous live recording would be a chart-topper. And that left Darcy with a literal million-dollar question.

Who gained the most from Derek Tufnell's untimely demise?

Chapter Ten

The following day, Darcy was back at the record store. After spending so much of the previous one talking to people who may or may not have been completely straight with her, she'd passed the evening hours discussing the case with Ringo. While he'd been attentive, he hadn't offered her any helpful suggestions.

His relative silence had allowed her to walk through the case, though. That, in turn, led to a productive session at the suspect board in her office. She finished just in time to open the store as scheduled.

"Time to make sure the lights stay on." As she strolled through the store to unlock the front door, a familiar face came into view. It was Todd Robinson.

"What up, dude?" They exchanged a fist bump as she held the door open for him. "How are you feeling?"

"A little better. Been listening to Derek pretty much non-stop." He looked around the store as he poured himself a cup of coffee. "You all alone today?"

"Char's at the dentist, and I didn't want to ask Hank to come in on his day off. I figured if I can't handle the store solo for a couple of hours, I need to get a different gig."

They exchanged a laugh. Todd was in tech support for a local hospital. These days, he did most of his work from home. Often, when he was caught up on his assignments, he headed to the record store for a change of scenery. A lot of regular customers came in at predictable times—after work, on the weekend, or during their lunch hour. Todd showed up pretty much any time the store was open. The guy loved music like the way billionaires liked their money.

On this morning, Darcy was especially happy to have the company.

"We got a lot of Derek's music in yesterday. I was going to put it out this morning. Give me a sec, and you can have first dibs."

She fetched the crate from the office. Char had done her a solid. When the merchandise arrived the day before, she got it ready for the sales floor. Now, all Darcy had to do was bring it out. The inventory work was a task that Darcy handled when Eddie was still around. As much as she missed Eddie, it was heartening to see her team evolve.

"Here you go." She placed a crate of LPs and a box of CDs on the sales counter. "Have at it. Got a few imports in there you might like."

"Whoa." Todd pulled out a rare double album of a live concert performed in West Berlin in 1988, mere months before the fall of the Wall. "This is too cool. I've heard about this album. Supposedly a legendary show. Ninety bucks is a little steep for me, though."

"Tell you what." She looked around the store to make sure they were alone. "You've been a good friend to the store for a long time. How does half off sound?"

He smiled. "Looks like I picked the right day to come see you."

"Hey, what are friends for?"

It cheered Darcy to utter the words. For so many years, she'd been without friends. Then, even after she'd built solid friendships, she was still reluctant to use the term. Fear of slipping back into her former destructive behavior had been a wall between her and the people she cared about. Something impenetrable and insurmountable. It kept her safe. It isolated her, too.

It hadn't been until the days after solving Eddie's murder that she realized just how many people truly cared about her, checkered past and all. How many of those people wanted her to know they were her friends. And how, finally, after so many years of isolating herself from others, she'd dismantled those walls and become comfortable using the word that was so simple and yet so powerful, too.

Friend.

Todd gave her a fist bump. "Along that line, I've got news for you. I've spent a lot of time on Reddit commiserating with people about Derek's death.

There's a lot of chatter that he was drinking and giving women a hard time again."

"Is that so?" She kept her tone neutral. She had nothing against the social media site. It didn't change the fact that the threads were often as reliable as a weather forecast in Indiana.

"Totally. His drummer and tour manager are women. The situation was bad and getting worse. I thought you should know for your investigation."

"What makes you think I'm still investigating?"

"Word gets around. Especially because you were seen at the B & B talking to Derek's guitarist."

"Touché." She chuckled. "I love saying that word. It makes me sound so fancy. Anyway, word is correct. I'll follow up on your tip. If you hear anything else, let me know."

"You got it." He took a drink of his coffee. "If you don't mind me asking, why are you doing this? I mean, I totally get it last time. This time, why not leave it to the cops?"

It was a good question. Thanks to the toxicology report, Darcy was in the clear. After taking a couple of days to cool off, she was over her anger at how Detective-Sergeant Rosengarten treated her. Any rational person would totally understand if she chose to step aside and leave the investigation to the police.

Nobody in Marysburg, Indiana, would confuse Darcy with the word rational, though.

"Yeah, it is nice to not be suspect number one anymore. I need to do this for a couple of reasons. One, I've heard the same rumors you have. I owe it to the women he assaulted to find out the truth." It was more than rumors, but she wasn't going to share Gwen's story. It wasn't hers to tell. "Two, I understand the dynamics of a touring band better than anyone around here outside of Derek's squad. There may be something I'll notice that someone who hasn't lived life on the road will miss."

Todd nodded. "I can see that. Is it safe to assume you haven't offered to work with the Marysville P.D. in an official capacity?"

Darcy snorted. "Yeah, no. If they ever ask for my help, I'll gladly give it.

I'm not going to hold my breath, though."

"That's what I thought." He gave her a fist bump. "Good hunting. Do us all a favor and try not to get shot at, okay?"

"Deal." With a laugh, she rang up the sale. She could joke about having a gun pointed at her by a murder suspect now. Six months ago, it hadn't been humorous at all. There was a valuable lesson there, though.

Wherever the investigation took her, Darcy was going to have to tread carefully. And watch her back. Well, her front, above her, and below her, too. One couldn't be too careful when searching for a murderer.

By the time Charlotte arrived, Darcy was getting worried about her. "You okay, girl? Your cheek looks puffy."

"I'll be fine." She rubbed a spot on her face that was swollen. "They ended up having to put in a temporary crown instead of just a filling. Gonna stick to soft foods for a day or so."

"Can I go on a smoothie run for you? I mean, if you're up to covering the store solo for a bit."

Charlotte plopped down on the stool behind the cash register. "Sounds good. Can you make sure they don't make it too thick? I don't want to have to fight with anything right now."

"Your wish is my command." Darcy gave her a salute and fetched her bag from the office. "Back in a flash. And you are hereby ordered to stay seated and take it easy until my return. I'm playing the Boss Card."

A sandwich shop that also served amazing smoothies had opened in town three months ago. Darcy loved it. And loved, even more, the fact that it was only two blocks from the record store. Two recent grads of Ball State's Hospitality and Food Management program owned Sunny's Sandwiches. It offered four different kinds of bread, including gluten-free, and sourced as much of its offerings as possible from local growers.

Darcy loved to shop local.

She ordered a banana and blueberry smoothie for Char and a pineapple, grape, and almond one for herself. While she was waiting for her order, Chris Van Hoy came in.

Chris was a good guy. In addition to running the facility, he also acted as a handyman, head ticket taker, and sound engineer. In a pinch, he wasn't averse to making popcorn. He wasn't above taking out the trash after an event, either.

After exchanging greetings, Darcy asked him how he was holding up.

"Not going to lie." He ran his fingers through his graying brown hair. "It's been tough. I've got mixed feelings about Tufnell. I feel so bad for his family. And his crew...."

That was Chris in a nutshell. His first thoughts were about others. Back in the day, Eddie had supported hiring Chris to run the Marysburg. His current words were proof he'd been the right man for the job. Talented and compassionate. You didn't go wrong with people like that.

"I've spoken to some of them. They're struggling but hanging in there. How about you?"

"Haven't slept much. Whenever I close my eyes, I start thinking about things I could have done. But, no. Derek went off on me, and I let my feelings get hurt. Then, to find out, he was hit over the head and poisoned. At my facility. What a nightmare."

"Who told you he was poisoned?" Darcy didn't suspect Chris for a second. However, the authorities had been so tight-lipped about Derek's cause of death. It was eyebrow-raising that he knew about it.

"Paul Gerard. Saturday afternoon, he showed up with some other cops. They went through the trash and asked me a bunch of questions about beverage service the night of the show."

"Like what?"

"Where we got our beverages, who had access to them, what we gave the band. Stuff like that. It was annoying because we provided the band and crew complimentary beverages, but not Derek. He had his own fancy water. Ours wasn't good enough."

The woman behind the counter called Darcy's name. Her order was ready. She had so many questions with so little time.

"You said he went off on you. What was that about?"

"I was at the soundboard, doing my usual run-through before the sound check. Derek came storming over to me, saying I needed to let his sound tech run the board. He was a real jerk about it. It made me mad. If he wanted his own guy on the board, fine. There was no need for that."

"I'm so sorry you're having to deal with this. Do you have some time to come with me to the record store? There are a few more things I'd like to ask you."

He placed his order, then gave Darcy a nod. "After what you did for Eddie, it's the least I can do."

Darcy smiled. Solving the murder, with Eddie's memory right beside her, was the least she could do.

Chapter Eleven

A few minutes later, Darcy and Chris entered the record store. Charlotte was finishing up a sale of two cassette tapes to a young man wearing a Ball State Baseball T-shirt and matching cap.

"I can't believe people are actually buying those," Chris said when the customer had left the store.

"It's a niche product, for sure." Charlotte took her smoothie from Darcy as she gestured toward a small set of shelves filled with cassette tapes. "Gotta give the people what they want. Right, Boss?"

"Truth." Darcy took a sip of her smoothie. "If someone as big as Billie Eilish is willing to put their music out in that format, we'll sell it."

"In that case, I've got a bunch of old cassettes at home I haven't listened to in years. Interested in taking them off my hands?"

Darcy looked toward Charlotte. Buying pre-owned merch became one of Char's duties when she was made the store's general manager.

"Bring them by. Can't promise anything, but I'll be happy to take a look." She gave Chris a business card.

"Sweet." He turned to Darcy. "What was it you wanted to talk to me about?"

Here was a chance to find out if Brian had lied to her. "You said Derek insisted on using his own sound engineer and board."

"Yeah. I tried to tell him we have a state-of-the-art system, but he wasn't going to listen to me. So, his engineer brought in his own board, and I spent the show looking over his shoulder to make sure nothing disastrous happened."

"Okay. Do you know if they recorded the show?"

"Yeah. The sound engineer was an okay guy. He apologized for Derek being a jerk and told me they were recording the show, so everything had to be perfect. That's why they had to use their own equipment and people."

Darcy did a little drum roll on the sales counter as she processed the information. It elicited more questions. Did Brian really not know the show was being recorded, or was that a big fat lie? If it was a lie, what was the point of doing so?

"Makes sense, but Derek's producer said he didn't know anything about a live recording."

"Would someone in his position know about that?" Charlotte took a long slurp of her smoothie. She was making it disappear like she hadn't eaten in weeks. "I mean, I thought he was only in town to wish Derek good luck."

"If you ask me, Brian McGuinness wasn't in town to wish Derek luck," Chris said.

"Why not?" Darcy and Charlotte asked the question in unison. In recognition of that, they exchanged a fist bump.

"During the show, he and a woman were hanging out by the soundboard. She was a real looker. And probably half his age. At one point, he told her that Derek was worth more dead than alive."

"Holy smokes, Chris." A jolt of electricity shot through Darcy. "Did you tell the cops?"

She shook his head. "To be honest, I forgot about it until right now. He laughed after he said it. I got the impression he was showing off. Must have worked because he and the woman took off like twenty minutes into the show."

And yet, he'd been in the green room with Derek after the show. Where, exactly, had Brian been up to during that two-hour gap? It was a question that seemed crucial to the investigation. Darcy couldn't wait to corner the producer and ask it. That would have to wait, though.

"I think you should let Officer Gerard know. I'm sure the police would be interested in that piece of information." Darcy's mention of Paul rather than Kaitlin was intentional. The Detective-Sergeant had made it crystal clear that she viewed Darcy's efforts as an impediment. If the woman was going to be that way, Darcy would still cooperate, but in her own way.

Chris looked at his watch. "I need to go. The community theater has rehearsal in an hour."

Darcy gave him a fist bump. "I appreciate all your help. Will you be there around six? I'd love to pick your brain some more."

"Sure. Like I said, anything for the woman who caught Eddie's killer."

The rest of the afternoon flew by. With Charlotte on register duty, Darcy kept herself busy by going through the vinyl to put misplaced albums in their proper spots. When Izzy arrived for her shift, Darcy asked her to do the same in the CD section.

A little before six, Darcy threw her bag over her shoulder. "Char, take it easy. I'll do the trash in the morning. If you want, you can leave the deposit for me to do that, too."

"Heading somewhere, Boss? Like maybe on a date with Liam?" Izzy giggled as she gave Darcy a light punch on the arm.

"I wish." She and Liam had been friends for years. This new stage of their relationship was as scary as it was exciting for Darcy. Because of that, they were taking things slow. If anyone asked about the relationship, she said they were dating.

She wasn't ready for a boyfriend. Though, when she reached that stage in her life, Liam would be a pretty good choice.

"I'm going by the Marysburg. I want to have my own look around."

"Keep your eye out for murderers." Izzy gave her a hug. "Supposedly, they always return to the scene of the crime."

It was good advice. "I'll keep my eyes peeled."

* * *

The theater troupe was wrapping up rehearsal when Darcy entered the theater. It was working on a presentation of *Beauty and the Beast* for the holiday season. Based on the little bit Darcy caught, it was going to be an excellent show.

She joined Chris at the soundboard. "Thanks for letting me do this. Do you mind if I wander around?"

He shrugged. "Sure. Looking for anything in particular? The cops were pretty thorough."

"I don't know. Guess I'll know it when I see it. One question before I get started. When did the tour bus arrive?"

"I got a text from Vanessa when they got into town. The driver was having a little trouble finding us." He checked his phone. "They got here a couple minutes after eleven."

"Thanks. That's super helpful."

With her hands in her pockets and her mind open, she wandered off. First, she went to the concession stand. Since Derek was poisoned, it seemed logical enough to start where drinks were served. After all, someone spiked his flavored water. Maybe the deed had been done there.

She ran her index finger along the top of the spotless glass counter. It was similar to the one at Marysburg Music. Instead of valuable, music-related collectibles, this one was with boxes of candy and sweets. Her stomach rumbled when her gaze came across a package of red licorice.

"Shush," she said to her belly, then laughed. It was good nobody was around to hear the embarrassing reaction to the candy. It was her second favorite, falling just short of the divine treat of pretzels and Nutella.

After taking a moment to appreciate the pristine condition of the popcorn machine, she moved to the soda machine. It served the usual—water, lemonade, cola, diet cola, and root beer. No flavored water. None of the hoses appeared to be tampered with. It had been a long shot, but the devil was in the details. That meant she had to be thorough.

Next up for examination was a small fridge behind the counter that housed a selection of bottled beverages. Beer and wine took up most of the space. On the bottom rack, though, she came across bottled flavored water.

"What do we have here?" Before her brain could take off like an LP being played at 45 speed, she closed her eyes and took a deep breath. Once she was centered, she took a close look. The brand was a common one. She saw it in the drinks section whenever she was at the grocery store.

None of Derek's water was to be found. Well, the concession stand search had been worth a shot. The police hadn't missed any key clues. It was likely whoever poisoned Derek didn't do it here.

The rehearsal had ended while Darcy was checking out the concession area. Actors and crew were milling about in front of the stage. Darcy slipped into an empty seat next to Chris. She handed him a twenty-dollar bill.

"What's this for?"

"The red licorice. Love it." She opened the package. "Feel free to keep the change. You can call it a donation."

He rolled his eyes. "Find anything the cops missed?"

"Sadly, no. I noticed y'all stock flavored water, though. Is there any leftover from the water Derek was drinking?"

"No. The contract asked for six bottles of a specific, high-end brand. The smallest quantity I could order was twenty-four. I didn't want to have to do that, so I agreed to reimburse them for the cost if they provided it themselves. After some grumbling, they agreed."

"Yeah, sounds like Derek. Back in the day, he drank his flavored water with healthy doses of booze. I can't help wondering if he was doing that again. You mind if I look around some more?"

"Be my guest. I'll be here for another hour or so." He raised his eyebrows. "You really think you'll find something the cops missed?"

"You never know. The sooner I get this solved, the sooner we get this place out from under the black cloud hanging over it."

"Then don't let me keep you."

The green door was closed. That star with Derek's name was still affixed to it. A shiver went down her spine when she grasped the doorknob. It was cold to the touch. She took a deep breath before entering.

"Focus. You're not chasing ghosts. You're looking for evidence."

The room was much the same as she'd last seen it. A throw pillow sat at one end of the couch. She recalled seeing another one. It must have been removed during the investigation. Perhaps it was in evidence, along with Derek's award.

The window caught her attention. It was closed, which made sense since it was late October. She crossed the room to get a better look. The lock, which was engaged, gleamed in the light cast by the overhead LED fixture.

In fact, it was so shiny it looked brand new.

She grabbed a sturdy, wooden end table and climbed up onto it. Once she was eye level with the window, she released the latch. With a push from her index finger, it swung out from the bottom.

"Interesting."

The window frame was about three feet wide and two feet high. Levers with mechanisms at either end of the frame allowed one to lock the window in an open, horizontal position. If the window was open, someone small could sneak in through the opening. Provided they could reach the window.

Cameron wasn't a large man. He was about Darcy's height and looked to weigh thirty or so pounds more than her. Someone with those measurements could squeeze through and make some mayhem.

"Find anything?"

The question caught Darcy so off guard she almost fell off the table. Sending a death glare at Chris, she righted herself and leapt to the floor. Her heart rate was beating faster than the drums, the classic surf tune "Wipeout."

"Holy smokes, Chris. You scared the daylights out of me." She put her hand over her heart and took deep, cleansing breaths until it stopped banging against her ribcage like a drumstick against a bass drum.

His cheeks turned crimson. "Sorry about that. Things are quiet out front, so I thought I'd check in."

"Tell me about the lock on the window." She might as well put his presence to good use.

"Had it put in yesterday. The old one didn't work so great. It's been on my to-do list for a while, but I never figured someone would actually sneak in through it. It's a good ten feet from the ground outside."

"The window was open the night Derek was murdered." She drummed her fingers on the table. "Any chance someone could have used the window to sneak in and then stayed out of sight in a restroom or, I don't know, a utility closet?"

"I suppose it's possible." He dropped onto the couch. "Did you know someone emailed me and wants to buy this? Offered ten grand. The buyer wants to include it in a Derek Tufnell Museum."

"Okay, that's creepy." She wrapped her arms around herself.

"No doubt. The Center could use the money, though. Ten grand would help pay the license fees for next season's Civic Theater performances. I have a meeting with the Board members tomorrow night to discuss it."

They were getting off-topic. On top of that, Darcy had a cat who probably thought he was starving she needed to get home to.

"Getting in through the window was possible, though, right?"

"Yes, but it was locked the night before. I know because I did a walkthrough to make sure everything was ready for the show."

"So, if someone did get in that way, most likely it was part of an inside job, right? Since someone obviously unlocked it."

"Probably. If that's the way it went down, then the poisoner was working with someone in Derek's group. It doesn't necessarily mean the person who came through the window, if someone actually did, was part of the group."

Darcy leaned against the table, hating what she was about to say. "Or the poisoner is one of the band or crew. And the window doesn't factor into the murder at all."

"But what about Tufnell getting whacked on the head? And that guy with the songwriting beef who was hanging around?"

"Those are good points." She rubbed her hands together. "I don't have answers to either of those questions. I promise you, though. I *will* get them."

It was a promise she intended to keep. With so many moving pieces, the question was how."

Chapter Twelve

The next morning brought a mix of sun and clouds. The temperature was forecast to reach the mid-sixties. Marysburg, Indiana, didn't get weather much better than that in the third week of October.

"Looks like another day for a ride to work, buddy." She gave Ringo some fish that was left over from her dinner the night before. "Eat up. Supposed to be good brain food for us humans so it can't hurt you. Right?"

The cat didn't bother looking up from his bowl the entire time he gobbled up his breakfast. When he was finished, he spent what seemed like ages licking his chops.

Darcy laughed. "I agree. That's some good stuff. And as a reward for putting up with me being gone so much the past few days, you can have the last of it tomorrow morning."

Ringo responded by giving her a *mrow* and rubbing his cheek against her shin.

"You're very welcome." She popped the last of a homemade omelet in her mouth and washed it down with some green tea. "Gotta go. Later skater."

She shrugged into a gray zip-up hoodie with the Marysburg Music logo on the back, set the alarm, and with her skateboard under her arm, blew her cat a kiss goodbye. It was going to be a good day. She felt it.

She pushed herself along the trail, smiling up at the sun as the hard-driving sounds of The Pretty Reckless came through her headphones. Darcy loved the band as a whole. The story of how the lead singer, Taylor Momsen, left a successful acting career so she could front a rock band was inspiring. That took guts.

It was early enough in the day that shadows enveloped Darcy when she reached a tree-lined section of the trail. It was her favorite part of the trip. She couldn't resist singing along to the rocker "Take Me Down." It had some killer drumming, after all.

As the song was coming to an end, from out of nowhere, a figure jumped out from the shadows. With the force of a rugby player, the assailant drove their shoulder into Darcy's midsection. Utterly unprepared for the attack, she went flying. She landed in a heap among the rocks and sticks alongside the trail. Her board rattled to a stop twenty feet from her.

The blow knocked the wind out of her and left her flat on her back in a daze for a moment. Stunned by the dual impacts, she lay on the ground and waited for her senses to return. The figure loomed over her. Their features were obscured by a dark hoodie pulled down over their eyes. They tossed a piece of paper at her.

"What the...?"

Before she could finish the question, her attacker took off, sprinting away for thirty or forty yards before cutting away from the path and disappearing among the Autumn foliage.

There was no chance of pursuit. Instead, Darcy shook her head to clear the cobwebs. She sat up, grimacing as a lightning bolt of agony shot through her lower back. When the pain eventually subsided, she got to her feet, picking up an earbud that had fallen out.

She looked up and down the path. Not a soul was to be seen. During the summer and on the weekends, dozens of witnesses would have seen the attack. At this time of the year, on a Thursday morning, not so much.

"Come on, man. Where's some help when you need it?" A blue jay perched on a nearby limb took flight without answering her. "Whatever, dude."

After a few moments spent massaging the bruised muscles in her back, she unfolded the mysterious piece of paper. The note written on it was short and to the point.

Drop the investigation. Now. Before you get hurt worse.

She studied the threat. It was hand-printed in black ink on a nondescript piece of letter-sized paper. There were no obvious giveaways to point to the threat's source, like the Marysburg Bed & Breakfast letterhead or a watermark from Derek's record label.

Despite her ongoing pledge to refrain from using vulgar language, she let out a string of curse words aimed at whoever wrote the threat. Sometimes a healthy frac, her go-to cursing substitute, didn't get the job done.

The next time she saw Peter, she'd ask for his forgiveness. They made a pact a while back when Darcy suggested he was using foul language more than needed. Language like that might come back to bite him during his auditions to get into college. They'd agreed to keep the cursing to an absolute minimum. Any violations would involve the offending party paying the other a dollar for each word used.

In the minutes that passed while Darcy was gathering herself back together, not a soul had emerged on this section of the trail. At least that meant nobody had been subjected to her tirade.

"Fine, whoever you are. I know a threat when I see one. I also have a long history of ignoring threats. So, watch out. I'm coming for you."

She took her phone from the pocket of her hoodie and texted Hank to let him know she might be a little late getting to the record store. There was someone she needed to have a chat with.

By the time Darcy arrived at the police station, the aches in her back had diminished. It was probably only temporary relief brought on by the skateboarding activity. He made a mental note to take some pain reliever as soon as she got to the store. This was no time to be sidelined by a stay in the emergency room. There was too much to do.

"Is Detective-Sergeant Rosengarten in? I need to report a crime."

The clerk covering the front desk looked up from his paperwork. His short, black hair was parted on the side in a classic military style. He gave Darcy a long look before rolling his eyes. Nonetheless, he picked up the phone.

The man, who Darcy didn't recognize was silent for a few seconds. "Detective-Sergeant, there's a woman here who wants to report a crime. She asked for you specifically."

After a few minutes, Kaitlin Rosengarten entered the reception area. Her smile morphed into a frown when she made eye contact with Darcy.

"What's this about a crime, Gaughan?" The detective crossed her arms and began tapping the toe of her black work boot.

"I was on the way to the record store. Someone knocked me off my skateboard—"

"I'm sorry to hear that. Accidents can happen if you're not paying attention to your surroundings. Reserve Officer Wayman can take your report." She turned to go.

"And left this note." Darcy raised her voice and thrust the piece of paper in Kaitlan's direction. "Threatening my life."

The Detective-Sergeant stopped in her tracks. Her shoulders sagged, but she turned around.

At her nod, Officer Wayman took the note. His eyes widened as he read its contents. "I think you should take a look at this, Sarge."

"That's Detective-Sergeant." She held the page in a corner with her thumb and index finger and gave it a quick read. "Come through, Gaughan."

Darcy followed Kaitlin to the same room where she'd been interrogated the previous Saturday. The cop took the same seat as last time. Darcy, in a display of defiance, grabbed a seat at the end of the table instead of sitting across from her.

"Let me make sure I've got this right. You were skateboarding to work. Someone knocked you off your board. Then they gave you this note." Kaitlin tapped her finger on the unfolded piece of paper.

"That's a serious oversimplification." Darcy closed her eyes and counted to ten. If she said anything more, the situation would fall apart, and Kaitlin would toss her in a holding cell.

She recounted the incident in as much detail as she could recall. About halfway through Darcy's report, the cop started taking notes. It encouraged her that Kaitlin appeared to be at least somewhat interested in the story.

"Other than someone wearing dark clothes wearing a hoodie pulled over their head, you can't give me a description of your alleged assailant."

Okay, maybe her encouragement was premature. "It happened so fast. One minute, I was fine. The next, bam, I was on the ground. They were gone before I had a chance to react. I apologize for not asking their name and address."

"No need to get snippy."

"I don't know." Darcy spread her arms wide. Frustration was settling in. "Maybe there is. Based on that note, Derek's murderer is still running around. Now my life may be in danger."

"Then, using your own logic, the answer's obvious. Stop putting your nose where it doesn't belong. Leave the police work to the professionals before I have to arrest you for interfering in a criminal investigation."

Darcy opened her mouth to fire off a witty retort but thought the better of it. Getting into another argument with Kaitlin would only help Derek's murderer. That's what she needed to focus on.

"Fine. Do you want the note or not?"

Kaitlin stared at it for a minute, then tossed her pen on the table. "It could be someone playing a prank on you. Or it could be of value. We'll hold onto it."

A cool wave of relief washed over Darcy. She sat back. If she was going to be honest with herself, the incident had scared her as much as it had made her angry. Her injuries were minimal. This time. Next time she might not be so lucky.

"Thank you. I appreciate it."

"You never know. It might come in handy." Kaitlin stood. "For what it's worth, we took Cameron Jessup into custody for violation of a restraining order Mr. Tufnell had against him. It's a moot point now, but it gave us a chance to question him."

This was huge news. Darcy maintained her poker face, though. After talking things through with Chris, she was ninety-five percent convinced Jessup wasn't the murderer. A conclusion the police should have arrived at, too. The fact that Kaitlin shared the development piqued her curiosity.

"Did he offer you any helpful information?"

"Maybe." She smiled. It had the menace of an apex predator. "A letter was found in his possession. He alleges it was from Mr. Tufnell, inviting him to a meeting after the show. He was instructed to enter through the back door.

And to keep the meeting confidential."

"Have you been able to verify its authenticity?"

"We've shown it to Mrs. Tufnell. She said it looks like the deceased's handwriting to her."

"Can I see it? You know, to compare the handwriting. Maybe the letter was a ruse to lure Jessup here. What if the letter and my note were written by the same person?"

"I'm afraid I can't allow that." She opened the door. "I've got your contact information if we need to get in touch with you."

On her way out, she noticed Paul Gerard. He was at his desk, sunglasses perched on his head, looking at a computer screen. She cleared her throat.

"Hey, Paul. I mean Officer Gerard. How's it going?"

"Busy, but okay." He got up. "I was about to go on patrol. I'll walk out with you."

"Isn't your car parked in back?" Paul was a good guy. Darcy's distrust of the authorities ran deep, though. Thus, her initial distrust of the offer.

"My wife says I could use the steps." He chuckled as he patted his belly, which seemed plenty flat to Darcy. "Don't worry. I'm not going to bust you for anything."

Once they were outside, she let out a long breath. Her entire body tensed up whenever she entered the police station. It was a conditioned behavior left over from her days when she'd been hauled in via the back doorway way too many times.

Darcy turned into a breeze coming from the south. It warmed her face and provided a moment of tranquility.

"I overheard you came in to report an assault. Are you okay?"

Paul was the polar opposite of Kaitlin. The Detective-Sergeant eyed Darcy with constant suspicion with a healthy serving of disdain on the side. The patrol officer always displayed compassion first. Questions came later.

Sure, he'd joined the force after Darcy had entered rehab, while Kaitlin had arrested Darcy more than the rest of the current police officers combined. Still, Darcy had proven she deserved the benefit of the doubt these days. She'd moved on from her dark days. Why couldn't Kaitlin do the same?

"I'm good. The back's gonna be sore for a while, but that's about it. More shaken up emotionally than anything. I'm glad I had my phone in my hoodie pocket instead of my jeans pocket."

"Thank goodness for small favors." He kicked a pebble from the sidewalk onto the street. "It sounded like you think your incident's related to Mr. Tufnell's murder."

"I don't think it. I know it." She told him about her conversations with the members of Derek's entourage. "His murder was an inside job. I'm convinced of it. The murderer obviously didn't like me having those conversations. If I could get a look at the letter Jessup had on him and compare it to mine, that would help."

"How so?"

"If the handwriting is the same, it stands to reason they were written by the same person. Either the murderer or an accomplice, maybe."

Paul scratched the collar of his uniform shirt. "It's an interesting theory. Of course, I can only talk about hypotheticals since I'm not assigned to the case. And if I was, I couldn't talk to you about it."

"Fair enough." She set her skateboard down. "Here's something else for you to consider, hypothetically, of course. "I'll admit I didn't get a good look at the person who attacked me. I got a good enough look to bet my life that whoever it was, it wasn't Cameron Jessup. They were too tall."

"And how would this information help the investigation, hypothetically."

"Where is Jessup now?"

"I think he has a hearing today. Why?" Before Darcy could answer, Paul nodded. "Jessup couldn't have been your assailant because he was in custody at the time of the incident."

"And the real murderer might not know that. I'd bet you a soda pop the murderer wrote Jessup's letter as a way to lure him to the theater." She nodded as the picture in her head became clear. "Derek was already dead by the time Jessup snuck in through the window. The real murderer set him up to be the patsy, figuring everyone would accept the idea that he whacked Derek on the head. They didn't count on a toxicology screen being done."

"So, we're dealing with someone who's not exactly the sharpest tool in the shed."

"Totally." She held up her index finger as a new thought came to her. "Or maybe someone who's too full of themselves. You know, the kind of person who thinks they're smarter than everyone else."

Paul nodded. "Interesting thoughts. I appreciate you sharing them with me. I promise the Detective-Sergeant and her team are working the case as hard as they can. Like fourteen-hour workdays. They've gathered a lot of evidence, and it takes time to go through all of it."

"Is that a nice way to tell me to back off?" Darcy gave him a light punch to his arm to keep the mood friendly.

"As a police officer, I will always tell you to leave work like this to the professionals. It's for your own safety, after all." He returned her punch with a gentle squeeze of her elbow. "As someone who lives here, I have a feeling you're not going to let anyone tell you what to do."

He tipped his baseball-style cap to her and walked away.

Darcy stood there for a moment, contemplating Paul's less-than-cryptic parting words. She laughed. Here she was, in front of the very building that was a real-life House of Horrors. Now, it was a place where she had allies. Her number one ally was no other than Paul Gerard. Not so long ago, he'd trained his service revolver on her. Today, he was sharing information with her.

With a shake of her head, Darcy pushed herself in the direction of Marysburg Music. My, how things had changed in a matter of months.

* * *

She was in her office catching up on some paperwork she'd been ignoring for a few days when her phone dinged. It was a text from a number she didn't recognize. The message was short.

Hope this helps

An image was attached to the text. She debated opening the file. Clicking on links in emails and text messages was a super easy way to get caught up in a ransomware attack. With the investigation going on, though, something in the back of her mind encouraged her to open it.

She clicked on the link. And took in a breath when she figured out what she was looking at.

"Holy smokes. I must have a guardian angel in high places."

The image was a high-resolution photo of the letter the police obtained from Cameron Jessup. The handwriting was identical to the note her assailant had left with her.

Chapter Thirteen

"Hank. Check this out." Darcy jetted from her chair as a burst of adrenaline flowed through her.

"What in the world?" His trusty feather duster had come to a stop in a corner of the store by the ceiling, as if it had been hit by a stun ray. "Are you okay?"

The treads of her sneakers let out a loud squeak as she came to a stop by his side.

"You're not gonna believe this." With her heart banging away at speed-metal pace, she handed him her phone. She drummed her fingers on her thighs as he put on his reading glasses to study the photo on the screen.

"Help me out. What am I looking at?"

"It's the connection I've been looking for." She brought him up to speed on her conversations with Kaitlin and Paul.

"Wait a minute, young lady. Why am I just now learning you were accosted on the trail?" He gave her a look, complete with furrowed eyebrows and a frown, which would have made the Hall of Fame of disapproving parental expressions.

"Because I knew you'd react exactly the way you are right now." She bumped her shoulder against his in a show of friendly affection. "I'm fine. I've got a little soreness, but the only thing that got really hurt was my pride."

"Hold that thought." A man entered the store, so Hank went over to greet him. When he assured Hank he was just looking around, Hank returned to Darcy's side.

"Where was I?" He snapped his fingers. "Right. We can discuss the significance of the picture on your phone after we discuss the ramifications of what happened to you this morning."

"I told you I'm okay. I ripped the pocket of my jeans when I hit the ground. That's all." She wandered over to the cash register when the customer picked out a copy of Beyoncé's latest album. Queen Bey music never remained in stock for long. To Darcy, that was the way it should be.

"For now." Hank followed her. He kept his voice low to avoid attracting the customer's attention. "Let me ask you this? How did your attacker know you were going to be on the trail this morning?"

Two college-aged women entered the store before Darcy could respond. As Hank turned on his heel to greet them, a sarcastic response died on her lips. The man had a point.

She'd been focused on so many other things. The confrontation, then the note, then the revelation of Jessup's arrest, and finally, the mystery text. She hadn't taken time to step back and take a good hard look at the circumstances surrounding it.

It wasn't simply a matter that it happened. It was a matter of when and where it had happened. It had been planned. Just like Derek's murder had been planned. A chill ran down her spine.

Somebody was watching her.

The refrain from the Police hit, "Every Breath You Take," popped into her head. The tune sounded like a love song when given a casual listen. That was the point, though. Once one paid attention to the lyrics, the song's menace became impossible to miss.

She put her hands on the sales counter as her chest tightened. Her lungs constricted, making it almost impossible to draw breath. Her ears began ringing. She felt like she was being stung by an entire hive of bees.

"Darcy, what's wrong?" Hank's question was muffled, as if it had been asked from the other side of a solid wood door.

"Panic..." She tried to suck in some air, but her windpipe was like a storm drain clogged with fallen leaves. "Attack."

Hank put his arm around her and guided her into the office. Once she was seated at her desk, he dug his phone out of his pocket.

"Close your eyes." As she did so, the calming sound of ocean waves filled the room. "Take deep breaths. I've got it covered out front."

Darcy did as she was told. It took what seemed like decades and a lot of focus. Eventually, her lungs relaxed, and she was able to breathe freely. A few minutes later, she opened her eyes. The walls were no longer closing in. The discomfort from the millions of phantom bee stings had subsided.

The panic attack had run its course.

It was the first one she'd had in two years. Even during the stress-filled days following Eddie's murder, she hadn't experienced one. Though, that was probably because her mind was too busy focusing on keeping the store open and solving the case.

As she massaged the muscles in her neck, she knew what she had to do. Keep her mind busy. Find something else to focus on for a while.

Like the case board behind her. Currently covered by a blanket, she'd barely worked on for a while. Now was as good a time as any to change that.

After a quick review of the information already on the board, she updated her suspect chart. Unless something completely unexpected developed, like a confession, Jessup was out. She drew a line through his name. The same went for Chris. Not that he was ever a suspect, but she'd put his name on the board since he was at the theater early enough to fit the poisoner's timing requirements.

That left Derek's group.

"Let's see. We have a wife he was cheating on, a drummer he was sexually harassing, and a producer looking to do a documentary and live album. That gives me three suspects with motive."

The tech and other band members didn't seem to have motives, so Darcy drew lines through their names. She left them on the board, though. Just in case.

With the lineup of suspects narrowed, she turned her attention to the timeline. She used the metadata from the pictures she took during Derek's appearance at the record store and at the concert to fill in some of the time gaps between when the bus arrived and when Derek was found.

There was a knock at the door. "I take it you're feeling better?"

"Much. Thanks." She handed Hank his phone, then gave him a tight hug. "Having you and the rest of the gang working with me makes me the luckiest boss ever."

"It's nothing." He gave her a few pats on the back. "We take our cues from you. Your board looks different. Progress?"

"Some. Trying to narrow the windows of when the murderer was able to give Derek the poisoned water."

"Good work. Holmes would be proud of your scientific approach. I hate to interrupt your work, but a merch order just arrived. Most of it's Derek Tufnell music."

She put down her marker. "Awesome. Let's get it priced and on the floor ASAP."

They prepped the merchandise for sale between pauses to help customers. Traffic picked up as the day went on. A fair number of Derek's albums were purchased by the time Peter clocked in at three.

"Holy Mother of Music," he said with wide eyes while admiring the display honoring Derek that had been assembled. "I had no idea there was so much love for the dude."

"I remember when David Bowie passed away." Darcy looked at a poster of the Thin White Duke on the wall opposite the cash register with a smile. "We hadn't been open very long. It was just Eddie and me back then. For a week, practically every customer who came through that door wanted Bowie music. It blew us away."

Hank scratched his elbow. "I still have a hard time wrapping my head around the fact that his estate sold his music catalog for 250 million dollars. I get that he was a legend, but, wow."

Peter went behind the register to ring up a sale. "That's nothing. Did you hear about Springsteen? He sold his for half a billion. I wouldn't mind being one of his kids, oh yesi."

"Any idea what will happen to Derek's catalog?" Hank asked.

"Depends on who owns it." Darcy straightened a stack of albums. "If Derek did, it would go to his wife. If he signed the rights over to his record label, then the company would hold onto them. Derek was no Bowie or

Springsteen, but I'd bet his catalog might be worth thirty or forty million."

Peter let out a low whistle while Hank put his hand over his heart.

"That's a lot of coin." Peter shook his head.

"And a lot of motive for murder." Hank tapped his finger on one of Derek's CDs.

Darcy sighed. "Which means I need to figure out who owns the rights to his music."

"How you gonna do that?" Peter pulled his phone from his pocket, as if he was ready to run a Google search.

"The old-fashioned way." Darcy did a drum roll on the young man's shoulder. "By asking people in the know."

* * *

A few hours later, Darcy rolled to a stop in front of the bed & breakfast. On her way over from the record store, she'd worked through her list of people who would know about the ownership of the Derek Tufnell music catalog. Brian McGuinness and Sophia Tufnell were the most logical choices.

The question was how to broach the subject without making them clam up. It was a topic that would require tact and delicacy. Darcy wasn't known to have either. As she traversed the sidewalk to the front porch, she wished Char was by her side for this.

"You'll just have to keep your cool. You can do this."

She'd warm up with someone else, the keyboard player, Hamilton Barclay. Hambone, as he was commonly known, was the last member of Derek's original band still working with him. Their first record together, *Almost Midnight*, came out in 1971 to rave reviews. Over the next fifty years, Derek released twenty-two studio albums and four live albums with Hambone at the keys. Many had commented that Derek had been more faithful to his keyboardist over the years than to his wife.

They weren't wrong.

If anyone would know about the details of Derek's catalog, it would be Hambone.

Gwen was hanging out in the parlor. Darcy waved to her as she approached. She might as well ask one of her prime suspects a few more questions while the window of opportunity was still open.

"Hey, girl. How are you doing?" She took a seat in a leather chair catty-corner from Gwen's spot on a matching couch.

"Ready to go home." She closed a book she was reading, *#FollowMe For Murder*, by Sarah E. Burr. Darcy had read a few of the author's books and thought she belonged on the book bestseller lists.

"Any idea when that will be?"

"I'm going to give them until Sunday. If they haven't caught the murderer by then, I'm out of here. I can't afford to hang out and wait. Not with bills to pay."

"I hear you. And I'm sorry you have to deal with cash flow issues on top of everything else." Darcy drummed her fingers on the chair's arm. Most professional musicians were like folks with nine-to-five jobs. They weren't rich and needed enough income to keep the lights on at home. That often meant working another job when they weren't on the road.

Gwen and the rest of the band and crew were losing out on opportunities to make money every day they were stuck here. A tour insurance policy payout would take time to process. That was time that Gwen, at her young age, probably didn't have. It was real-life purgatory in every sense of the word.

"I heard you're doing your own investigation. That true?"

"I'm doing some poking around." Darcy leaned closer to her fellow drummer. "I was blown away when my name was leaked as a suspect. At first, all I wanted to do was clear my name. It's become bigger than that, though. Derek might have been a lowlife, but his murderer deserves to face justice. If I can help make that happen, great."

"Can you really do that?" Gwen brushed a few strands of hair from her face. "I mean, you're not exactly a professional investigator. No offense."

Darcy held up her hands. "None taken. Thing is, I've been where you and the rest of the band and crew have been. I know what it's like to live life on the road for months at a time. The dynamics of a tour bus are nothing new to me."

Gwen nodded. "Go on."

"I imagine there was a pecking order on the bus. After Derek, Hambone got first pick for sleeping quarters, didn't he? And maybe had input on the set list that the rest of you didn't have. Am I right?"

"Yeah. So what? Those two had been together twice as long as I've been alive."

"I understand the lifestyle better than the cops do. Don't get me wrong. They're smart people." She'd keep her real opinion of Detective-Sergeant Rosengarten to herself since she was talking to a suspect. "The issue is whether they know which questions are the right ones."

Gwen leaned forward. She'd taken the bait. "So, what are the right ones?"

"For example, who stands to inherit Derek's music catalog? That involves a sizable income going forward. Or, who stands to gain musically now that this tour is canceled and they're suddenly available?"

Gwen leaned back. "Those are good questions. I was just a hired gun. I don't know anything about Derek's finances. Just what's in my contract. For all the good that does me now."

"Fair enough. Thanks for the time." Darcy got up. It was time to back off. Sure, Gwen had plenty of reason to strike back at Derek. But to murder him? Unless her life was in danger, that seemed excessive. Especially with folks who had stronger motive still in the picture.

"FWIW, last time I saw Hambone, he was in the back yard. You know, in case you want to have a chat with him, too." She used her fingers to make air quotes when she said chat. "I'm not sure where everyone else is."

"Point taken. I'll pay him a visit."

Darcy wandered back outside, then around the side of the building toward the six-foot high wooden privacy fence that surrounded the back yard. She was about to open the gate when a man's angry voice made her stop.

"I don't care that you think it's a tall order. I want those numbers first thing tomorrow morning." There was a pause, like the man was on a phone call. "I've waited long enough." More silence.

Darcy opened the gate enough to peek into the back yard. Hambone, dressed in his usual black jeans and V-neck T-shirt, was pacing back and forth, taking a pull on a vape pipe every two or three steps. He stopped pacing and scratched the top of his head.

"Listen, every day this gets delayed is a day that I stand to lose money. That means you lose, too. Got it? Good." He jabbed the screen of his phone with a finger to end a call, blew out a massive cloud of vapor, then fell into a chair, most of which was out of Darcy's line of sight.

"Holy drum roll, fans. What has Derek's oldest friend gotten himself into?"

Staying on her tiptoes while hoping her question hadn't been overheard, Darcy slipped away. With potential scenarios swirling in her mind, she sped home on her skateboard. She was savvy enough to know that drawing conclusions from only half of a conversation was unwise.

Still, as she weaved around a young couple pushing a stroller, she let various set-ups run through her mind's eye, like a series of music videos. By the time the refurbished fishing shack that Darcy called home came into view, one conclusion was obvious.

A lot more people were unhappy with Derek than was widely known. The question remained. Which one was unhappy enough to do something drastic about it?

Chapter Fourteen

Fridays were always busy days at Marysburg Music. For a lot of folks, it was payday, which meant they had disposable income to spend on music. For the college students, it was the day to kick off the weekend festivities with new party music, especially since this was Ball State's Homecoming weekend.

Since Izzy and Peter were seniors at Marysburg High School, a sizable portion of the teen set had started hanging out at the store before going to the football game or other activities.

In short, the little record store that Eddie and Darcy had nursed through infancy had grown up into something much grander than she could imagine back in the day.

Marysburg Music had become cool. In fact, it was one of the places in town to see and be seen. And not just among music lovers. People with all kinds of interests came through the store's front door, often with big smiles and open wallets.

Of course, it didn't hurt that a local celebrity worked there.

"How many people have asked to take selfies with you today?" Charlotte gave Darcy the side eye after she handed a customer their purchase and told them to come back any time.

"I don't know. Half a dozen, maybe. It's Ball State's Homecoming weekend. A lot of people are in town for the first time in a while. You're not complaining about how busy we are, are you?"

"No way." She shook her head. "Brisk sales are good for my job security. I just worry you're going to start putting the pictures of yourself and big shots on the wall of the office."

"Or worse, on the walls out here." Izzy exchanged a high five with Charlotte as she handed a sale to Darcy to be rung up. "Can't have the big boss getting a big head."

"Are you a celebrity?" The customer, a heavyset man with thinning hair and glasses, reached for his front pocket. The typical place for a dad or grandpa to keep his phone.

Darcy smiled and shook her head. "No."

"That's a lie," Charlotte said. "She was a drummer in an influential punk band, and singlehandedly apprehended a murderer here in town last spring."

With cheeks getting as hot as the burners on her gas stove at home, Darcy forced a laugh. "I love my co-worker here, but she likes to exaggerate."

"It's not an exaggeration." Liam came up beside the customer. He pointed to his phone screen. "Here you go, my man. Check out this news report about her."

The customer's eyes grew wide as he read the article. "Wow. My granddaughter's a sophomore at Ball State. I remember her parents talking about this. For a while, they were worried about her."

"She's got nothing to worry about." Liam pocketed his phone. "With people like Darcy here, the area is as safe as any place in America."

"Um." The man's Adam's apple bobbed up and down. "I heard there was another murder around here. Are you sure about that?"

Darcy cleared her throat. "The police are working diligently on the case. Given the circumstances, there's no reason to believe there's a local connection to the murder."

"What's that mean? No offense, I'm just I'm concerned about my granddaughter's safety. Comes with the territory of being a grandparent."

"None taken. I get it. As a matter of fact, I was talking with the police about the case yesterday. They have a number of promising leads they're pursuing. We believe the murder was committed by someone who had access to Mr. Tufnell that the general public didn't have."

"An inside job, then?"

Darcy hesitated for a moment. She wanted to put the man's concerns at ease. On the other hand, she didn't want to say anything that could come back to haunt her. She didn't know this man, after all.

"I used to be a touring musician." She pointed to the Pixie Dust poster on the wall. "I have an understanding of a touring band's inner workings. A member of the community wouldn't have been able to get close enough to Mr. Tufnell to murder him the way he did."

"You seem pretty confident about that if you don't mind my saying."

"Trust us," Charlotte said. "Darcy knows her stuff. Both with the music biz and as a crime fighter."

"Okay." He shook Darcy's hand. "You all convinced me. I'll set my worries aside."

When the man stepped away, Liam rubbed his hands together. "I feel like we should get Team Gaughan, P.I. shirts or something."

"Please don't." Darcy covered her face with her hands. She'd made progress with her comfort level as the face of Marysburg Music. Beyond that, it was still a struggle.

"Can I take you out for a late lunch at Selena's, then?" Liam draped his arm over her shoulder. "I'm buying."

"Go on, Boss." Izzy gave her a gentle push. "We got this."

Darcy's buddy Thea hadn't reported to work behind the bar, so she and Liam took a table by the window in the main dining room.

While they munched on tortilla chips and salsa, Liam brought her up to speed on the latest drama at the auto service center.

"I'm telling you, I never thought putting together a work schedule would cause so much angst. One of my techs threatened to quit if I didn't give him tomorrow off so he could go to the Homecoming game."

"That's one of the reasons I love my team. The only schedule drama we had was when I had Char start doing it. She was afraid to ask me to cover when both Peter and Izzy needed to be off for music commitments. I told her not to worry about it. I love every minute I spend at the store."

"Color me jealous."

"Well, it's going to be tough replacing Peter next year." While the young man still needed to audition, Darcy was certain he would have no problem being admitted to Indiana University's Jacob's School of Music to study music performance. She'd worry about his replacement when the time came.

They took a moment to give the server their orders. When they were alone again, Liam asked how the investigation was going.

"Making progress, but it's slow." She told him about her recent conversations. "I didn't want to say too much to the guy at the store, but I have no doubt someone from the band did it."

"Who's at the top of your suspect list?"

"For now, I think the whole thing comes down to money. Whoever owns the rights to Derek's catalog stands to benefit the most, so I'm thinking that way."

Liam cracked his knuckles. "You know, that makes me think of something. At the concert, remember when I went and hung out with Chris for a while?"

"Yeah, you said you were going to play rock star."

"Right. So, I was standing next to Chris, and there was this older guy hanging around. He was with a total smoke show who looked about half his age. I remember him saying he knew Derek. That his best days were behind him."

"Really? Chris told me he overheard something similar." Darcy ran through her suspect list in her head and mentally moved Brian to the top of the list. "I don't know about you, but I thought he sounded great. He looked good, too."

"Same here. That's why I forgot about it. I figured he was just some old dude trying to get lucky with a younger woman by acting all important."

Darcy scooped some salsa onto a tortilla chip. An idea was forming in her head. It was a long shot. Still, what was the old saying? Fortune favored the bold, or something like that? There was no better time to be bold than the present one.

"What did this guy look like?"

"Let me think." They were silent while their server placed their orders on the table. "Shorter than you and thin. Gray hair. He had on this massive watch. Probably some luxury brand I couldn't pronounce. Oh, and he was wearing a scarf. I thought that was pretty over the top."

The hunch was paying off. She allowed herself a small smile. On the day of Derek's murder, she'd seen a man wearing a scarf and a large, luxury watch. That man was none other than Brian McGuinness.

"If I'm right, I know who you're talking about. It was Brian McGuinness. He was Derek's producer." She chewed on a forkful of arroz con pollo. The savory chicken made everything in Darcy's life better.

"You wouldn't expect a producer to talk bad about his client, would you?"

Darcy shook her head. "Normally, no. It wouldn't make sense. Unless he knew something that nobody else did."

Liam took a sip of his water. "Like what?"

"That Derek was only hours from his death."

Chapter Fifteen

Darcy was in her office reviewing sales receipts for the past few days when there was a knock on the door. After a glance at the Rolling Stones clock on the wall, she let out a groan. It was time for her monthly check-in with the man who had been her property owner for a short period of time, Rafe Majors.

The man had inherited the building that housed Marysburg Music after his stepfather Eddie Maxwell died. In a move of unexpected generosity, he chose to sell the building to Darcy for a price significantly lower than real estate developer Todd Meadows had offered him.

That move had scuttled Todd's plans to build a condo development on the site. And made Rafe public enemy number one to a number of pro-business elements in town. Despite his slacker reputation, he'd come into his own in the months since Eddie's murder. He was working more hours at his library job and had a goal of applying for a full-time position the first chance he got. He'd even come to relish his new status as someone who used the prosperity from his inheritance to Stick It to The Man.

To make sure he was able to keep sticking it to the man, he met with Darcy to make sure he was taking care of his money.

Darcy didn't mind helping him with his finances. Partly, she felt good helping Eddie's stepson. It was a way to keep paying her mentor back for all the kind things he'd done for her.

On a more practical note, Rafe had sold the building to her on contract. If he got into money trouble, the vultures would start circling. There was no doubt in her mind that Todd or one of his minions would jump at the chance to buy the contract from Rafe.

They'd say it was a way to help him get out of his financial difficulties. What they wouldn't mention is that they'd give the ink a drum beat or two to dry, then move to resurrect the condo plan. That, in turn, would force the record store out. Was that a likely scenario? No. Was is possible? With Todd Meadows in the mix, anything was possible.

Especially with money involved.

That's why Darcy tolerated the monthly check-ins. It bugged her to no end that they had to happen at seven P.M. on a Friday since she preferred to be out on the sales floor. He claimed it was the only slot he had available. Since it was common knowledge he spent his Friday nights enjoying the area's bar scene, there was an unspoken understanding between them that he used the meeting as a launching pad for his partying.

They needed each other, so she accepted the situation as a cross she had to bear.

"Come on in, Rafe." She opened a spreadsheet on her laptop while he got settled in one of the guest chairs.

"Haven't seen you since our last meet, D.G. An eligible lady like you should be out and about. Where've you been hiding yourself?"

He considered himself to be quite the heartbreaker. Darcy didn't have the heart to correct him.

"Same old, same old. When I'm not here, there are always projects at the cabin." She glanced at the computer screen, not in the mood for idle chit-chat. "The store payment went out on the fifteenth. Did you get it?"

"Yep." He gave her a big smile. "Proud to say I haven't touched it yet."

"Excellent."

Since Rafe had inherited Eddie's house and car, both of which were paid off, he was virtually debt free. Darcy had convinced him to use the money from his part-time job at the Marysburg Library to cover living expenses like groceries and utility bills. That way, he could put the record store payments into a savings account and build himself a nest egg.

"Last month, you told me you were going to talk to the gas and electric companies about moving to budget plans. Have you done that?"

Rafe's smile disappeared. "Do I really have to do that? I got plenty of money, right?"

Spirits above, give me strength, please. Darcy looked down so he couldn't see her roll her eyes. Despite the progress he's made in recent months, Rafe had a long way to go to become self-sufficient. When faced with a task that he thought was inconvenient, he simply ignored it.

Darcy knew all too well from her drinking days that avoidance never worked. If anything, it only allowed an issue to build upon itself until it was a problem. She didn't want that to happen to Rafe.

"The money in your bank account isn't the issue here. It's getting colder. Your gas bill's going to jump big time once you start using the furnace. You don't want to find yourself scrambling to come up with an extra hundred bucks or more every month."

"Fine, I'll do it first thing Monday." He dictated a note into his phone to set a calendar reminder. "Now, when you gonna catch that guitar player's murderer?"

Darcy sat back in her chair. The reaction was much the same as when she first heard about Robert Plant and Alison Krauss collaborating. Things had worked out smashingly on that partnership, though. Maybe Rafe could shed some light on Derek's case.

Rafe had always been the type of person who didn't concern himself with events that didn't affect him personally. Like the murder of a musician, he wasn't a fan of. Well, it couldn't hurt to give the man a chance.

She removed the blanket from the suspect board.

He got to his feet, his stare never wavering from the information she revealed. First, his brow furrowed, then he frowned. After a while, his eyes grew wide.

"Did you do this when you were investigating the old man's murder?"

"I did."

"Man, you're not playing, are you?" The question carried a respectful tone Darcy had never before heard from Rafe.

"Nope. The cops have their approach." She tapped the whiteboard with her finger. After her conversation with Liam, she'd added photos of the suspects to the board. "I have mine."

"How can I get in the game?" He sat back down.

"First off, it's not a game." She waited for him to nod before she proceeded. "Second, if you really want to help, tell me what you know about the night in question and/or the people in the pictures."

He was quiet for a while. Then, he stepped closer to the board to get a good look at the pictures.

"I remember her." He pointed at Sophia Tufnell. "She was at The Lounge last Friday with some dude. Who is she?"

"The murdered man's wife." Sophia had been out with another man the night in question. That was noteworthy.

"Huh. Don't they always say when someone's been knocked off, look that the spouse or whatever first?"

"They do." Darcy added a note to the board regarding Sophia's whereabouts. She had to give Rafe credit. His information was helpful, even though when he gave her a description of Sophia's companion, no bells of recognition went off. "Do you remember what time it was when you saw her?"

He flipped his phone over in his hand as he pondered the question. It was the latest generation iPhone. The man loved his shiny toys. It didn't change the fact that it pleased Darcy to see him taking the issue seriously. For as long as she'd known the man, the only thing he put any effort into was his gaming. This behavior was a welcome change.

"We pre-partied at my place for a while, then had dinner and drinks at Selena's. By the time we got to The Lounge, it was around nine. I remember because we were yanking Jaime's chain about his girlfriend texting him asking when he was going to be home."

"This is really helpful, Rafe. Thank you." She added the fact to the timeline. Not only had Sophia been out with another man, but she also hadn't even stuck around for the show. It was odd since her surprise arrival had been supposedly so she could be there for her husband.

"Any idea how long she was there?"

"Nah. We were busy watching an MMA fight."

It had been worth a shot. Regardless, the information he provided filled in some holes. It also forced an issue Darcy had been hoping to avoid—having a chat with Sophia. She'd need a whole tour bus's worth of tact if she was going to get anything out of the woman.

Plus, Darcy didn't know where she was staying. Or if she was even still in town. One step at a time, though.

"I really appreciate this, Rafe. Do me a favor. Ask your buds if they remember anything about her, will you?"

"Sure thing. Gotta protect my property value now that I'm a homeowner. Know what I'm saying?"

"That I do." She walked him to the office door, cringing on the inside as she did so. It was just like Rafe Majors to find a way to be helpful and yet still have the case be all about him. At the end of the day, he'd helped. That's what mattered.

"Survive your monthly torture session," Charlotte asked Darcy the moment Rafe stepped outside. There was still a good number of customers in the store. She was happy to give her boss some good-natured ribbing now that Darcy was back on the sales floor.

"It was good, actually. He's got a ways to go, but I think he's making progress." Darcy took a Nicki Minaj album that had been left out and slotted it back in its proper place.

"Without his safety net, it's not like he has much choice."

"True. I wish Rafe had made these strides while Eddie was around to see them. It would have made him proud."

A woman with rainbow accents in her hair and a dozen used albums in her hands approached the register. In response to Char's raised eyebrows, the customer laughed.

"I'm deejaying a party later. Need to replenish my supply of records to scratch."

"Nice haul you've got there." Darcy peeked at the stack. The records were all dance music from the eighties.

"Sweet." Char extended her fist for a knuckle bump. "If you want, add your deets to the board over there. We get one or two calls a week asking if we know any deejays."

"No way. That's so cool. I'll do that." She tucked her purchase under her arm and made for the information board. Once there, she tacked a business card to it. Then she waved goodbye to them.

"Look at you. Building bridges within the music community." Darcy put her arm around her friend. "Eddie would be proud of you, too."

"Don't tell anybody, but the music community is a lot more fun to be around than the accounting community. They're nice people, but still...." Charlotte was a CPA by trade but had left the field because of burnout. As general manager of Marysburg Music, she was able to add her love of music to her skill with numbers. That had resulted in an improved bottom line for the store. And better sleep for Darcy, knowing the store was in good financial hands.

* * *

Once the final customer of the day had left, she grabbed Charlotte by the arm and shared Rafe's information with her. "I've been dying to tell you but didn't want to say anything in front of anyone we don't know."

"Wow. Paranoid much, Darc?"

"Until I figure out who knocked me off my skateboard, I don't think so."

Charlotte stopped counting the bills in the cash register. "That's fair. More to the point, how does his intel help your case?"

"It makes me wonder why Sophia didn't stick around for the show when supposedly her whole reason for being in town was because of Derek."

"Okay, but didn't you say that she wasn't exactly filling the room with good vibes? I mean, what if she knew that he was up to his old shenanigans and wanted to throw it in his face by hooking up with some rando?"

"Coming all the way here from the East Coast just to stick it to him? That's cold." Darcy shuddered at the thought. The level of animosity that much effort would require was disturbing.

"Lifestyles of the rich and famous." Char hummed a tune while she finished the night deposit. "Do you think she was in town early enough to be the murderer?"

"Until I know more, it's possible. To be honest, coming here to knock him off makes more sense than showing up for a revenge shag. And I'm sure he knows how much Derek liked to drink that flavored water." She rolled her neck to release some built-up tension. "You know what all this means, right?"

Charlotte twirled her index finger in a circular motion. "Go on. Don't keep me in suspense."

"I need to talk to Sophia Tufnell before she leaves town. And gets away with murder."

Chapter Sixteen

After spending all day with the activity level turned up to eleven, Darcy decided she'd start off Saturday taking things slow. For her, the best way to take a breather was with a tasty breakfast at her good buddy Jenna Washburn's diner. Excellent food with one of her besties. That was a chart-topping duet.

"Hey, Darc." Jenna waved at her from behind the dining counter and pointed toward a stool at one end.

As was usually the case on Saturday mornings, the diner was busy. Servers laden with orders moved from the kitchen to tables with fast-paced efficiency. More importantly, every one of Jenna's staff was smiling.

It was a testament to their boss. Jenna fostered an atmosphere where the staff felt valued. Where, provided you held up your end of the bargain, whether it was in the kitchen, serving customers, or bussing tables, she would always have your back.

That same combination of iron will and boundless optimism is what Jenna relied upon during the time she and Eddie got Darcy back on her feet. It was the unwavering belief in Darcy's ability to change, even during the worst of times, which had gotten the former drummer through the darkness and to the point where she was now.

Darcy would never be able to repay Jenna for all that the woman did for her back then. The least she could do was eat at the diner on a regular basis. And make sure Jenna had first dibs on all ABBA music and memorabilia that arrived at Marysburg Music.

"How goes it, Madame Blanc?" Jenna put a cup of steaming hot water and a packet of green tea on the countertop in front of Darcy.

"Who?" She opened the packet and dropped the tea bag in the cup.

"Madame Blanc. It's a mystery show on Acorn. The main character is an art expert who turns to amateur sleuthing when her husband dies under mysterious circumstances. Come over sometime soon. We'll binge it together." She leaned over the counter to get close. "Maybe you'll pick up a tip or two to help with your investigation."

"Sounds good to me." She scanned the menu. Jenna was always trying out new things by putting them on the menu as daily specials. One of the limited-time offerings caught her eye. "How about the Belgian waffle with strawberries?"

"Good choice. I've gotten a lot of positive feedback on them. Sprinkle of powdered sugar on top?"

"Yes, please." Darcy chuckled. She was going to need all the sweetness she could muster when she had her talk with Sophia. First, there was a little detail. She needed to find the woman.

When Jenna returned with her order, Darcy held out her phone.

"Before you go, does the woman in this picture look familiar to you? Like, maybe she's eaten here, or maybe you saw her around town recently?"

"I don't think so. No, wait. She was in here a few days ago to get a takeout order. Who is she? Should I know her?"

"It's Sophia Tufnell. She's the wife of the murder victim. I'm trying to track her down so I can talk to her. Did she mention where she was staying, by chance?"

"Afraid not. She was on foot, though, so she must be staying someplace within walking distance. At least, she was then. Gotta go."

While Jenna took care of her customers, Darcy munched on her breakfast. The golden-brown waffle was crispy on the outside, with a texture inside that was lighter than air. The subtle sweetness was a perfect complement to the to-die-for strawberries.

Between sips of her tea and bites of her breakfast, Darcy studied a map of the area on her phone. The Marysburg House was the only place that offered lodging in town. Derek's group had all the rooms booked there. Sophia was staying somewhere else.

"Where are you, Mrs. Tufnell?"

"I know you were asking that rhetorically, but have you considered she's staying someplace she found on Airbnb?" Jenna raised her hand for a high five. "You can thank me later."

The suggestion proved to be worth its weight in a dozen gold records. By the time Darcy finished her breakfast, she'd found eight homes online that were available for short-term rental. Four of them were located within a mile of the diner. That was tolerable walking distance for someone who looked as fit as Sophia.

She transferred the addresses of the top four to the notes app on her phone. As she did so, she couldn't help wondering how people obtained information before the Internet. While the net was a source of plenty of bad stuff, she was thankful for all of the good things to be found there, too. Like cat videos.

And locations where a prime murder suspect might be staying.

"Breakfast was amazing, Jenna." Darcy dropped three ten-dollar bills on the counter. She owed the woman her life. She would tip well for the rest of her life. "I'll let you know how the search goes."

One of the homes was on her way to work. She hopped in her battered Jeep she lovingly called Rusty, and turned the ignition. The engine rumbled to life without a single beat of hesitation.

"Way to go, Gina." She patted the photo of her hero, Go-Go's drummer Gina Schock, taped to the dash. The ritual brought her good luck. Liam insisted that even though it was over a decade old, if she gave it the scheduled maintenance he recommended, it would last her another decade. She was happy to do as he instructed. And would take all the luck she could get to go with it.

He was a good-looking guy with a heart of gold and was good with his hands. That was Darcy's kind of trifecta.

A few minutes later, she approached the first house on her list. It was a single-story ranch with an attached two-car garage on a large plot of land. Oaks and maples towered over her, their leaves bursting with color in vibrant shades of orange, red, and yellow. The manicured front lawn was a swath of deep green that reminded her of the greens at the Marysburg Country Club.

She pushed the doorbell, then spent the next few moments in borderline panic mode as she debated what to say if Sophia opened the door. The anxiety was replaced by disappointment when a young man with slicked-back black hair and brown skin opened the door.

"Hi." Darcy gave him a quick wave. "Is Sophia Tufnell here? I was hoping to have a few minutes of her time."

"Nobody here by that name. Sorry." He closed the door before Darcy could thank him.

Rejection wasn't a new thing in Darcy Gaughan's life. What was new was how she handled it. Instead of getting down, she straightened the collar of her jacket and returned to Rusty with her head held high.

"One down. Three to go. I'm gaining on you, Sophia."

Approaching the record store, Darcy noticed a lone figure hanging out by the entrance. It wasn't an unheard-of sight. Often, when big albums were about to drop, like Beyonce's *Renaissance*, people would line up so they could get their hands on the prized recordings as soon as possible.

Nothing was being released today, so the individual's presence, two hours before opening time, sent Darcy's senses into high alert mode. Maybe she was just being paranoid. She shook her head as she slotted into her parking spot behind the building.

After the assault on the trail, a heightened sense of caution was good sense. Nothing more, nothing less.

She took out her phone and keyed in 9-1-1. If the loiterer was harmless, she'd put it back in her pocket. If they weren't, she'd hit send without hesitation and make a fast retreat back to Rusty. She'd come too far, worked too hard, to lose everything because of carelessness.

Coming around to the front side of the building, she lengthened her stride, intent on presenting an image of being in control.

"Hi, there. I'm Darcy, the owner of Marysburg Music. We don't open until…." The rest of her words died on her tongue as she slowed to a stop.

The person waiting at the entrance was none other than Cameron Jessup.

"Hi, Ms. Gaughan." He extended his hand in an offer to shake. "I know you're investigating Derek Tufnell's murder. I didn't kill him. Can I talk to you?"

Darcy kept her thumb over the phone's send button. She fought off a sinking sensation in her gut. She *so* didn't have time to deal with this crackpot.

"Listen, Mr. Jessup. The police know you didn't do it. I know you didn't do it, either. Why don't you go home and try to put this place out of your mind."

"Oh." He chewed on his lip for a moment. Apparently, he hadn't expected Darcy's response. Then he took a step toward her. "The song, though. If you'd be willing to give me a few minutes of your time, I can prove he stole it."

She flipped through her keyring to give her a moment to decide on a sensible way forward. On the one hand, she had a million things to do, like conducting a deep Internet search on Sophia.

On the other hand, Jessup had been at the scene of the crime. What if he'd seen something important? Just because the cops had arrested him on the protective order violation didn't mean they'd asked the right questions while interrogating him.

"I can give you fifteen minutes." She unlocked the door, sending a silent plea to the rock gods above that she wasn't getting herself into a hole she couldn't climb back out of.

She settled herself on the stool behind the register. The sales counter created a barrier between them that gave her a sense of security. With that came faith that she could keep the situation under control.

"Okay, Mr. Jessup, before we get to the song in dispute, I want to ask you about the night Derek Tufnell was murdered." She pulled up the letter Cameron had given the police on her phone. "You claim you received a letter from him. He wanted to talk to you."

"Yeah. It said to wait by the back door. I know I was risking a violation of the P.O., but it was a chance to finally meet with him face-to-face. With no lawyers to get in the way. I couldn't get a ticket to the show, so I hung around outside."

"The whole show?" She didn't know this guy. There was no reason to trust him. Not yet, at least.

"Yeah. The letter said he wanted to talk after the concert. To keep things on the low down, I was supposed to avoid being seen."

She glanced at her phone screen. So far, Jessup's story lined up with the letter. "What happened next?"

"I tried to score a ticket, but nobody was selling." He shook his head. "I saw you and your friends go in, by the way. I hung out until the show was over and the crowd had left. Then, when he never showed at the back door, I crawled through the window. Had to use a trash can to reach it."

"Let me get this straight. You admit to sneaking into the dressing room?"

"Yeah. I thought there was no other way I was going to be able to talk to him. It was a dumb idea, but I was desperate." He took a piece of lined notebook paper from a manila folder. "Here's the original lyrics. I wrote them when I was in college back in the eighties."

The lyrics weren't a word-for-word duplication of Derek's turn of the millennium hit "Keep on Knockin'." It was close, though.

"How do I know you didn't write this after the song came out? After all, you sued and lost."

He handed her another piece of paper and a cassette tape. "This is an affidavit from a forensic document examiner. It says right there, I wrote the lyrics before the year 1990, way before the song came out. Read it yourself."

"Look, Mr. Jessup, I was the main songwriter while I was in Pixie Dust. Poems and songs have been around as long as human beings have. Just because someone's work is similar to yours, doesn't mean they stole it."

"Then, listen to this." He jabbed his finger at the cassette. "Once you do, you'll understand why someone tried to frame me for Derek's murder."

Despite her misgivings, Darcy did as asked. The cassette case was scratched from years of being handled. The paper insert was discolored with age. It was the kind music lovers used to make their own mix tapes before CDs took over.

A few anachronistic souls were still devoted to cassettes. That's why there was a cassette player on a shelf behind the sales counter. She inserted the tape and pushed the play button.

They waited for the song to come on. Once it did, she recognized the melody. The tune was a bit faster than Derek's blues-heavy version. This rendition had a punk feel, almost ska, even.

The song's arrangement was simple. Along with vocals, there was a guitar and drums. Derek's version included keyboards and a brass section. By the time the song ended, their similarities were impossible to deny.

It reminded her of the copyright infringement case involving Led Zeppelin's "Stairway to Heaven." That matter had been resolved in favor of the legendary band. Not unlike Cameron's suit against Derek.

She returned the tape to him. "I'll admit, they sound a lot alike. But I don't know what to tell you. The court case is over, and with Derek gone, what else is there to do?"

He pointed his finger at her. "You nailed it. With Derek gone, he can't admit he stole the song."

"Wait a minute." Darcy put her hands up to give herself time to think. Memories from eavesdropping on a phone call came to mind. "Are you suggesting that Derek was murdered to prevent him from admitting that he stole this song from you? And as part of the plot, the murderer lured you to the theater to frame you?"

"Exactly." His smile revealed a few crooked teeth. The man could use some dental work. Dental work he could have had done long ago if Derek had given him appropriate songwriter credit for the tune.

If he had actually stolen it.

"Tell me what you found in the room."

"It freaked me out. His head was covered in blood. He wasn't moving. One of his awards was on the floor. It had blood on it, too. I figured he was dead and climbed right back out the window."

"Why didn't you call for help? For all we know, he might have still been alive. You could have saved his life."

He dropped his head in apparent shame. "I know that now. At the time, I panicked. I was afraid people would think I killed him in revenge for the whole song thing."

The explanation had a ring of truth to it. As someone who'd made plenty of poor choices in her life, Darcy understood the gut reaction to run away from a sticky situation. In the larger picture, though, something didn't add up.

"Why did you stick around town? From what I can tell, all that did was give the cops a chance to arrest you."

"It was a long shot, but I thought I'd try to talk to Hambone Barclay. Try to see if I could get him to see the light."

And there it was. Bells and whistles went off in Darcy's head.

"Did you do that?"

"No. I was trying to find out where he was staying when the cops picked me up." He let out a sigh that carried the weight of the world with it. "You still believe me, right? I didn't do anything to Derek."

"Yes. I know you didn't kill him." She took his hand in hers. "You've given me a lead for my investigation, though."

"Really?" He stood up straight. "Who do you think did it?"

"I don't want to say anything yet." She gave him one of the store's business cards. "I suggest you go home. Leave town right now. If I'm right, you're not safe here."

Chapter Seventeen

Darcy's conversation with Cameron had given her more to chew on than an entire bag of pretzels dipped in Nutella. Red Vines were great, but pretzels and Nutella would always be her favorite snack of all time. Since Saturday was the store's busiest day, she had to wait until Hank, Charlotte, and both of the kids arrived before retreating to the office.

She told them she had a call about purchasing a used record collection she needed to return. The high schoolers bought the excuse. The more experienced team members knew better. Darcy had turned over used music purchases to Char at the end of September. It had become a code used by the senior staff when Darcy didn't want to be disturbed but wanted people to think everything was fine.

In other words, something was up.

This something involved updating the suspect board. She drew a red line through Cameron's name. Then she rewrote Hambone's name without a line through. There still wasn't much to go on. Yet. Until she was able to figure out what Hambone's mystery call was about, his motive would remain blank. The means and opportunity were there, though, and as strong as anyone else in Derek's group.

The question of why remained. He and Derek had been together for over fifty years. They were a blues rock version of Hall and Oates. Nobody had spent more time with Derek over the years with Derek. Not even Sophia.

Darcy drummed her fingers on the desktop. Could it be as simple as that? Did Hambone murder Derek to keep him quiet about something?

Derek had been open about the fact that one aspect of the tour was to apologize in person to the women he assaulted. What if he'd planned on going beyond apologizing for that reprehensible behavior? And in doing so, would reveal something Hambone wanted kept quiet.

Like the fact that Derek did, in fact, steal Cameron's song.

That would be a massive bombshell. It wouldn't necessarily be a career-ending one, though. Derek had dozens of hits to his name. He could reach a settlement with Cameron. Then, he could probably have a publicist spin it to make him look like it was one of his other apologies.

The media would eat it up.

Some fans would be angry. No doubt about that. The majority would forgive him, though. That's what fans did, after all. They forgave their fallen heroes. Because they wanted to believe their favorite ballplayer or musician, or politician was a good person at heart. Everyone loved a good redemption story, too, whether in real life or in a mystery novel.

"First things first, girl."

She stepped away from the board to let her thoughts simmer a bit. The day had begun with Sophia Tufnell as the suspect to be researched. She needed to do that before she turned her energies toward Hambone.

With her laptop under her arm, she exited the office. The jazzy, pop melodies of Lake Street Dive's "Being a Woman" greeted her. She chuckled at the irony of the song's lyrics, given all that was going on in her life. The songwriter, Bridget Kearney, couldn't be more right.

Being a woman was, indeed, a full-time job.

"What up, Boss?" Peter gave her a high five as she passed him. He was brewing a fresh pot of coffee. "Trying out a Jamaican blend my cousin sent from the island. Wanna try some?"

"I'll stick to my green tea, thanks. How are your audition rehearsals going?"

He let out a long sigh, then laughed. "It's tough. I'm still struggling with two of the pieces. I promise I'll have them down by the time I have to submit my recording."

"I have no doubt about that at all." She gave him a pat on the back.

The admissions requirements for the Jacobs School of Music at Indiana

University were among the toughest in the nation. Three out of every four applicants were turned away. The process was rigorous, too. First, an applicant had to submit a prescreening recording. That's what Peter was currently rehearsing. Then, if the applicant did well enough on the prescreening, they were invited for a live, in-person audition.

There were other hoops Peter was going to have to jump through, too. He could do it, though. The young man had talent, drive, and the thing that was most important. He loved playing music.

"How are things out here?" Darcy settled onto a stool next to Hank, who was on register duty. Charlotte and Izzy were helping customers.

"The Homecoming game kicks off in an hour, so things are settling down from utter madness to typical weekend craziness."

"Why didn't someone come get me? I would have helped."

He patted her hand. "We know you're busy with your special project right now. The sooner you solve it, the sooner you'll be able to return to our lovable, laidback boss."

They took a break from the conversation to ring up a few sales. Business was, indeed, brisk. Darcy wrote a note about planning something special during future Homecoming weekends and pinned it to the corkboard behind them.

"The store comes first. It has to, you know that." She bagged a customer's purchase and handed it to them with a smile and a request to come back soon.

"I do." Hank handled the cash register like it was an extension of his body. The man might be in his sixties, but his fingers had the dexterity and speed of legendary flamenco guitarist Paco de Lucía.

"I also know that when news hits that the crime is solved, people will come out in droves to congratulate you and thank you."

"That's not why I do it—"

He put his hand that wasn't working the number keys. "I know that, too. Doesn't change the fact that they'll come here to do it. And when they're here, a lot of them will make purchases."

Darcy opened her mouth to argue. Once her brain caught up with her mouth, she closed it. Then she shook her head.

"You're a wise man, Hank." She put the purchase he rang up in a canvas tote the customer gave her with a heartfelt thank you.

"I have my moments. You don't survive thirty-five years in customer relations like I did without being able to read a room."

"And that is why you are Marysburg Music's Chief Audio Consultant."

"Will you two quit gabbing and get to work?" Charlotte winked at them as she escorted a customer to the sales counter. He was holding ten LPs. She was carrying a Marysburg Music T-shirt and three CDs for him.

Yes, Ball State Homecoming was a good weekend for Marysburg Music. This year's version had turned out to be the best ever, in fact.

The team was exhausted by the time Izzy locked the door at eight o'clock.

"Not gonna lie. I'll miss days like this." Peter was folding shirts and hoodies that had been left awry by the shoppers. "It was fun."

"That's because you spent all day chatting up people by the coffee maker." Izzy threw a shop rag at him. "Time for you to clean up the mess."

"She's got you there," Charlotte said.

"Can I help it that I have a magnetic personality?" He gave them a wide smile. "Tell people a joke, give them a drink, and they can't bear to leave the store without buying something. It's smart sales."

Darcy left the teens to their friendly banter to clean the restroom. It was the job everybody hated the most, so she did it for a few reasons. First, it was a chance to turn her brain off after a day of listening to, talking about, and selling music. She loved music, but by closing time, she was ready to tune everything out for a bit. It was also a way to show her team how much she appreciated working with them. It was a small gesture, but it was important for them to see her doing the "grunt work." She might own the store, but that didn't mean she was above doing whatever needed to be done.

She'd just finished cleaning the sink when she got a text from Jenna, her friend who owned the local breakfast diner. They'd made plans to get together at Selena's to catch up. Sophia was at Selena's. Darcy needed to get there ASAP.

"Hey, y'all. Just got a tip on a suspect. Gotta run. Would you mind finishing

130

up without me?"

The group exchanged looks. Finally, Char cleared her throat. "Did you finish the restroom?"

"Yes."

They let out a collective breath they'd been holding. Charlotte took a step forward.

"Since you finished your chores, you may go. Be careful."

"Make good decisions," Peter said.

"Text us when you get home." Izzy exchanged a high-five with Peter. "We don't want to be up all night worrying about you."

Darcy stuck her tongue out at them and made her exit. God love them all; even in the toughest of times, her team knew how to get a laugh out of her while taking care of her at the same time. She was a lucky woman.

She crossed her fingers in the hope she could keep that luck going.

She stopped for a moment inside Selena's foyer. The restaurant's fabulous aroma of spicy beef and sizzling grilled vegetables made her mouth water. If she could afford it, she'd eat breakfast at Jenna's every morning and dinner at Selena's every evening. Ringo might get lonely, though. Which was a reminder to cut the dawdling and get to the task at hand.

Thea and Jenna waved at her as she entered the bar area. There was no sign of Sophia.

"Am I too late?"

"Hey, girlfriend." Thea poured Darcy a glass of lemonade. "Take a load off. Our friend is in the restroom."

"Yeah, we've been chatting her up." Jenna took a drink of her amber ale. "She was here by herself. When the chance to give her someone to talk to came up, we took it."

"Here she comes." Thea put a basket of tortilla chips in front of Darcy. "Act normal."

"Yeah, as if that could ever happen," Darcy said through a mouthful of chips. Jenna snorted, and that got them all laughing.

The laughter hadn't abated when Sophia arrived. "I hope I'm not interrupting something."

"Nope." Jenna slid the chips in Sophia's direction. "Our friend here was just telling us a joke."

Thea introduced Darcy to Sophia, then stepped away to make the woman a gin and tonic.

"I remember you. We met the afternoon of Derek's concert." She extended her hand to shake. It seemed like an oddly formal gesture for the casual setting they were in.

"I'm very sorry for your loss." Darcy took Sophia's hand in hers. It was warm but dry and rough, as if she'd spent the past few days wringing her hands while forgoing any lotion. It was a condition she remembered from her early days in rehab.

"Thank you." She took a sip of the drink Thea placed in front of her. "I guess when it's your time, there's no cheating the hangman."

Thea raised her glass of water in salute. "That's one of my all-time favorite songs."

Darcy's horror at Sophia's apparently unfeeling comment subsided when she realized the words were from "The Hangman," one of Derek's early hits.

"To be honest, I never cared for it. So dark." She shuddered. Whether it was thinking about the song or her husband's departure, Darcy couldn't tell. "The royalties paid for our first house, though. So, there's that."

Darcy took a gulp of her lemonade. The drink was refreshing, and the tang sharpened her thoughts. Sophia seemed as cold as the drink in her hand. On the other hand, maybe this was the way she grieved. Or, maybe she wasn't grieving. Perhaps she was simply being honest about the man who had mistreated her for so many years.

"Having someone murder your husband, that's rough." Darcy's response was blunt. She had a sense Sophia was comfortable with blunt. "I mean, this is your second husband to die under mysterious circumstances, isn't it?"

The woman stared at Darcy for a moment as she swirled her drink with a straw. "It is. My first husband's death was eventually ruled a drug overdose. We were both so young. This time, here are a lot more things I have to deal with, including consoling my daughters. The coroner released Derek's body today. I'm flying him home tomorrow morning so I can begin funeral arrangements."

Darcy had learned about Sophia's first marriage during her research earlier in the day. She had hoped it would rattle the woman. With no such luck, she slid another chip into her mouth as the reality of the situation made itself clear. If she was going to make a move, it needed to be now.

"At least you can say you saw his last show. I hope that helps. A little, at least."

"It does. So many people have told me how incredible it was being part of that." Sophia smiled. "Yes, I can carry that with me."

"I hope you enjoyed it as much as my friends and I did," Thea said. She didn't know that Sophia hadn't been at the concert. Darcy hadn't had a chance to tell her that.

"Yes. It was very special." Sophia took a long drink and placed her glass down. It was almost empty.

Liar, liar. Pants on fire. Darcy made a mental note to give Thea a high five for setting the trap that Sophia walked right into. She wanted to see how far the woman would go to maintain the lie.

"I'm so sorry we missed you after the show. Derek was in such high spirits." Darcy shook her head in what she hoped was a display of believable sympathy. "What a shame."

"I have to admit, between traveling that day and the show, I was worn out when it ended. I went back to the house where I'm staying. Figured I would catch up with Derek in the morning. So much for that, huh?"

Another lie. Probably. Rafe had confirmed her whereabouts during the concert but not after. That would be easy enough to confirm, though. Either Sophia or the guy she was with would have paid their bill before leaving the Lounge.

Thea was tight with all the bartenders in the area. Darcy could count on her to help answer that question.

"I own the record store in town. For what it's worth, sales of his music and merchandise are through the roof across the world. Hopefully, that shows you how much he was loved. It ought to provide you with some amount of financial security going forward, too."

Jenna stared at Darcy with furrowed eyebrows. She was going to have to get over her displeasure with the line of questioning. Darcy needed to know where Derek's money was going.

"It will." Sophia yawned. "Derek wised up and started holding onto the rights of his music beginning in the mid-eighties. So many artists who were huge in the fifties and sixties have nothing to their names because someone else owned the rights to their songs. Shameful."

"Any idea who owns the rights to Derek's earlier music?" Jenna asked. Evidently, she'd clued in on where Darcy was going with the line of questioning.

"I don't. Brian was his producer for decades, so it wouldn't surprise me if he does." She asked Thea for another gin and tonic. "To be honest, I don't really care. I can take care of myself."

"Amen to that." Jenna clinked her glass to Sophia's. "Do the police have any leads on who did it?"

Sophia let out a laugh. "If they do, they're not telling me."

"I'm still trying to get my head around who would do such a thing," Thea said as she replaced Sophia's empty glass with a full one. "Do you have any ideas? I mean, sometimes it helps to vent in friendly company."

"Thea is as good of a therapist as she is a bartender." Darcy exchanged a knuckle bump with her. "If you feel like talking, we're here for you."

"Well, obviously, it's someone who knew Derek loved his flavored water. And could get close enough to his supply to spike it." She tapped her index finger on the bar top. "And spent enough time thinking about it to know how to poison him to death. And hated him enough to hit him over the head to make sure he was dead. Sorry, I've had a lot of time to think about it."

"No apology needed." Darcy put her hand on the woman's shoulder. It was a manipulative move, but there was a murder to be solved. And Sophia was still a suspect. "If there's one thing I know, it's how important it is to acknowledge our feelings, not bottle them up or ignore them."

"That's very kind of you to say. Especially since he was back to his old tricks. That hurt a lot. I probably shouldn't say too much, though. You all might start thinking I'm the one that knocked him off."

134

The group laughed. It was a natural reaction. A tension-releasing response. All the same, Darcy couldn't help wondering how many secrets Sophia Tufnell was keeping to herself.

And whether any of those secrets included murdering her husband.

Chapter Eighteen

Darcy's Sunday morning was spent cuddling with Ringo. With winds from the north bringing a blanket of gray clouds and cold rain, they hung out in the living room instead of on the deck that overlooked the river.

The cat, curled up on Darcy's lap, purred as loud as a lawnmower as she scratched his ears. With a big mug of hot tea sweetened with locally produced honey in the other hand, she scrolled through her case notes.

"Welp, buddy, one of my suspects is getting out of Dodge this morning, and there's nothing I can do about it." She scratched up and down his spine, which brought forth even louder purring.

"The thing I can't figure out is, why would she go to all the trouble to show up for the opening night show and then blow it off? Seems to me if she was in the mood to get back at him by finding someone to mess around with, she could have done that without the travel. Unless it was more than that."

The cat raised his head and stared at her. Then he put a paw on her hand.

"I know. I need to stop obsessing over Sophia and get to work. I can't afford to feed you if I don't have a job. And your kitty cat comfort is what should always be the number one thing on my mind. Off to work it is."

She wrapped Ringo up in the cotton throw that was covering her, got to her feet, and placed the cat, still wrapped up, back in the recliner. He flicked his ears and gave Darcy a *mrow*.

"You're welcome. See you tonight. Hopefully, with some answers. Later, skater."

As the day wore on, the weather improved. The drizzle ended midafternoon. By closing time, the clouds had dissipated, too. The remaining cool but clear conditions were ideal for an after-work walk to unwind.

"I'll take care of the bank deposit," Darcy said. "I'm in the mood for a stroll before I head home."

"No progress on the case, huh?" Charlotte handed her the bank bag.

Derek's murder hadn't come up all day. Once or twice, Izzy had opened her mouth to say something, but had closed it after exchanging a look with Char. Darcy had gotten the impression her team had decided to avoid the topic unless she brought it up.

It was a thoughtful gesture. One that had allowed her to enjoy the workday without being reminded of the black cloud still hanging over Marysburg. Now that the workday was over, the edict had evidently come to an end.

"Not really." Darcy gave her a summary of the conversation at Selena's.

"Do you really think Sophia's the murderer?"

"I don't know. Maybe. It's possible if she got into town soon enough to start spiking his drinks. At this point, I don't have enough info to rule her out. Holy smokes, there are still so many suspects."

"Which is why you're going for a walk." Char hugged her. "May your thinking time help you find some answers. See you in the morning."

After making the deposit, Darcy rubbed her hands together to warm them. The chill in the air was a reminder to get her gloves out of the storage box where she kept her cold-weather gear.

And that gave her an idea.

With a renewed sense of purpose, she marched to the Marysburg Center for the Performing Arts. This time, she wasn't going for another look around inside. She wanted to check out the surrounding neighborhood.

If her working theory was right, Derek's murderer was someone close to him. At some point, that person would have had to replace some of the flavored water with antifreeze. That led to three questions.

First, where did they perform that switch? Second, what did they do with the water they replaced? Third, what did they do with the container of antifreeze?

If the murderer was smart, they would have drunk the extra water and gotten rid of the container. But not someplace the police likely would search. On a hunch, she texted the number that had sent the photo of the Cameron Jessup note. It was a simple question.

Did the police find a container of antifreeze in their search at the Marysburg?

Within a minute, her phone pinged. The speed with which she received an answer surprised her as much as it pleased her.

No

Okay, then. That meant the murderer didn't toss it in the theater's dumpster or the trash cans by the front and rear entrances. Where did it end up?

Was it in a trash can somewhere on the route between Boston and Marysburg? It hadn't been stashed on the bus. Otherwise, the police would have found it, and the reply text would have had a different answer. What if it was still somewhere nearby?

"Think, Darcy." She came to a stop a block from the theater.

The building itself was flanked on either side by single-story buildings that housed a law firm and an insurance agency, among others. In the past, one of the storefronts had been home to an ice cream shop, another had been a shoe store.

No doubt, the decades-old buildings held countless secrets from days gone by. Did they hold any new ones?

Presumably, the murderer didn't have their own transportation. There were no rideshares in Marysburg, so that option was out. An absence of any length of time to dispose of the antifreeze jug could have been noticed. On the other hand, nobody would have given a second thought if a member of the group said they were going for a short walk to stretch their legs.

She began her search behind the buildings two blocks from the Marysburg Center for the Performing Arts. Forty-five minutes later, she'd looked in every nook and cranny within a two-block radius of the theater.

No luck.

She'd searched the blocks to the right, to the left, and behind the theater. As she drummed her fingers on her thigh, she mulled what to do next. All of her searching had been in areas the murderer could have reached via alleyways in order to stay out of sight.

The street that ran in front of the Marysburg Center for the Arts got a lot of traffic. Which meant a lot of eyeballs on it during a busy Friday. Surely, they hadn't dumped the container someplace that would have required crossing it. It would have been foolish to take that kind of risk. Crossing that street would have been asking for trouble.

Or a stroke of devilish genius.

"Where are you hiding?" She looked up and down the four-lane street. On the other side, to her left, there was a bank, a jewelry store, an Asian restaurant that made the best cashew chicken in the world, and an empty storefront.

"There." Thankfully, traffic was light since it was Sunday evening. She jogged across the street, then down a block to the vacancy. A sign in the window advertised luxury apartments from Meadows Realty were coming soon. After a look around to see if she was being watched, she slipped down the alleyway that ran alongside the future residential structure.

At the end of the building, she came to another alley that ran behind it. A light fixture above the vacant space's back door was empty. The darkness was palpable. Menacing. She turned on her phone's flashlight.

In response, something small scuttled away behind her, leaving a trail of oily-looking leaves in its wake. As if on cue, the wind picked up, which created an eerie whining sound.

A shiver went down Darcy's spine, followed by a second one.

"Let's make this fast, girl, before some maniac in a mask shows up."

She stepped into the deeper gloom directly behind the building. The circle of illumination the flashlight created was insignificant compared to the darkness and dank smell of decaying leaves and rotting food that someone had left behind.

At the base of the building, the flashlight's beam came across a section of wall that had started crumbling away. Something was jammed into a gap where the mortar had separated.

With a mix of fear and anticipation, Darcy crept closer. Fighting the dread that a rat would jump out at her, she extended her hand. The mysterious object was cool and smooth to the touch.

"Plastic."

It was wedged far into the gap. Whoever had jammed it in there had done a thorough job. A closer look with the flashlight confirmed the item was whitish in color. No, it was clear. She grasped what she could with her jacket sleeve over her hand her hand, took a breath, and pulled.

After a moment of resistance, it slid out with a scraping noise. Darcy let out a yelp as she fell on her backside, leaving the seat of her jeans soaked. The prize was in her hand, though.

The object was a clear plastic jug. One gallon in size. It had been smashed, but the label was still intact. She didn't recognize the brand name. That was okay. She recognized one of the ingredients.

Ethylene glycol.

Darcy allowed herself a small smile. "Ringo, I believe I found the murder weapon."

A moment later, she hit send on a text message. She didn't relish hanging out in a dank alleyway with who knew what lurking around, but there was no better opportunity to find out who her mystery ally with the Marysburg PD was.

It didn't take long to find out. Ten minutes later, a figure in dark clothes and a Ball State University baseball cap pulled down low on their head emerged from the shadows. "I hear you have something for me."

The voice was non-threatening. It was male. And familiar, too. Once Darcy's heart stopped beating a thousand beats a minute, she recognized the individual facing her.

"Thanks for coming, Paul." Since she wasn't in danger, her pride insisted she play it cool. "Glad you got here so quick. I can't wait around all night."

He raised the bill of his cap to reveal a grin. "The football game I was watching's a blowout. Didn't have anything better to do. What's up?"

"I was following a hunch and found this." She offered him the jug. "It was hidden in a crack over there. I'd bet a Pixie Dust gold record it contained the antifreeze used to kill Derek."

"Following a hunch, eh?" He slipped on a pair of surgical gloves. "Where'd you say you found it?"

She moved to the wall and pointed at the gap in the crumbling mortar. "Right here. It was smooshed in there good. Like someone was trying to hide it someplace where nobody would come looking."

"Except Darcy Gaughan, Private Eye."

He crouched down to get a closer look. He used a small flashlight bearing the logo of the Marysburg Police Department to probe the area. With a disciplined methodology, he alternated between photographing the spot in question and probing it with his fingers.

Then he removed a small plastic bag from a pocket and used it to hold tiny plastic shavings he dug out of the mortar. When he was satisfied, he got to his feet.

"Would have been better if you had texted me before removing the jug. Without these," he shook the plastic bag, "I would have only had your word that you found it there."

She bit back a snarky response. She'd just found evidence that the police had been unable to locate, after all. Paul had proven he had her back, though. Why ruin a good thing before it even had a chance to get off the ground.

"I get it. Integrity of the scene, and all that. In my defense, though, I didn't know who I was texting with. You could have turned out to be the murderer, like in the second season of *Only Murders in the Building*. Great show, by the way. If you haven't seen it, you need to."

"I'll watch anything that has Martin Short in it." He tugged at the bill of his cap. "You didn't know it was me who texted you that pic? Seriously? I thought you were a detective. I mean, I did slip you that detail about the cause of death."

Darcy put her hands on her hips. The jug was still dangling from her sleeve-covered fingers. "I'm not a detective. I'm a musician and business owner. If your Detective-Sergeant hadn't thrown me under the bus, I wouldn't have had to get busy to clear my name."

"Fair enough." He motioned for the jug. "Come on. Let's get out of here before we end up with the flu, or something worse."

Silence loomed over them, the only sound coming from the buzzing of streetlights until they reached Paul's car a couple of blocks away.

"What's next?"

He opened the trunk. "I'm going to request an evidence technician come and check for prints on that wall. Then, we'll do the same to the jug. If we're lucky, we'll find enough trace amounts of antifreeze to compare the components with what was found in the bottles we recovered."

"Sorry to ruin your night." She zipped her jack up all the way in response to a gust of wind. "Any way you can leave me out of this? I think we both know what will happen if a certain someone finds out."

"Yeah." He put the jug in an evidence bag. "I'm getting myself into a morally gray era, aren't I?"

"How about this? You could say since the game you were watching wasn't any good, you went for a walk. You heard a sound when you were walking past the building. You went to investigate, and the jug caught your eye."

"Not bad. I can work with that."

Darcy stood a little taller. It was gratifying that Paul was taking her efforts seriously. "Does this make me a confidential informant?"

He barked out a laugh. "Sorry. No, it doesn't. Trust me, you don't ever want to find yourself in a C.I. role. Will you be okay getting home?"

Apparently, the conversation was over. Well, she'd followed her hunch, and it had paid off like a hit record. Calling it a day while she was ahead made sense.

"Yep. I'm good." She pulled her keys from her pocket. She could use them in self-defense in case the murderer was still keeping an eye on her. "Do me a favor? Let me know if you find any fingerprints?"

"Good night, Darcy." He ticked away at a cell phone, then put it to his ear.

With a shrug, Darcy headed for Rusty. On the way, she went through a range of emotions. First, she was annoyed at Paul for refusing her question. Then she was worried about what Kaitlin's reaction would be if she found out about Darcy's involvement. By the time she arrived at the jeep, though, she'd settled on a strong sense of accomplishment.

She'd uncovered a piece of evidence that had been missing. It was also encouraging that she did, in fact, have an inside contact at the police department. Provided she didn't abuse the source, of course. Above all, she was pleased that the discovery that came from hard work and dogged determination.

It felt as good as the first time she listened to Pixie Dust's first album from start to finish. That had been a moment she thought was beyond compare.

When it was time for bed, she curled up with the latest Sarah E. Burr mystery in her hands and Ringo at her feet. She was going to enjoy the escape that following along with Hazel Wickbury and her Aunt Poppy provided, then have a good night's sleep.

She'd earned it.

And when the morning came, she'd figure out her next move. She had no doubt it would bring her closer to catching Derek's murderer. And that would be more satisfying than having a song hit the top of the charts.

Chapter Nineteen

Monday morning hadn't been without its frustrations. First, Darcy woke up to find Ringo had hairballed right smack dab in the middle of the kitchen floor. It only took a moment to clean up the mess, but it wasn't exactly a positive way to start her day.

She couldn't help wondering if it was a harbinger of bad things to come.

Then a customer had come in demanding a refund on an LP that he hadn't even purchased at Marysburg Music. When Darcy pointed out that the album still had a sticker from Barnes & Noble on it and she would offer him was in-store credit, he stormed out, shouting at everyone within earshot he would be leaving one-star reviews every place he could think of.

"At least you get tomorrow off." Charlotte bumped her shoulder against Darcy's as they leaned against the sales counter. The episode with the disagreeable man had taken the wind out of both of their sails.

"True. Got to get through today's Chamber of Commerce lunch first." She shuddered. "Man, I hate these things. I don't see how Eddie survived them."

"We've talked about you comparing yourself to Eddie. Don't go there. It's only an hour. Sit by Jenna, and the two of you can take turns whispering insults at Todd Meadows."

That got a long laugh out of Darcy. When it ended, she wiped her eyes. "Thanks. You have no idea how much I needed that."

"I live to serve." Char bowed from the waist. "I don't, really. Just thought I'd say it to make you feel better."

"Duly noted." She checked the time on her phone. "I need to get going. At least they're serving chicken parmesan for lunch. Good golly, Miss Molly, it tastes so good. Want me to bring you something if there are any leftovers?"

"Nah. Trying to cut down on the cheese intake." She put her hand over her heart. "My cholesterol numbers are a little high. The dentist trip was a reminder that I'm not twenty-one anymore."

"I'm glad one of us is paying attention to things like that." Darcy shrugged into her jacket for the walk to the meeting. "If I'm not back by two, send out a search party."

It wasn't that Darcy didn't appreciate the Marysburg Chamber of Commerce. She did. The group had done wonderful things for her hometown and had taken measures to keep the local business community thriving.

She simply didn't care for hanging around a bunch of people in suits carrying on about things like income-to-earnings ratio and what the latest hot stock on the NASDAQ was. In her perfect world, people would attend these meetings dressed in jeans and T-shirts and discuss strategies for keeping the light bill manageable.

Such was the life of a former rock and roll rebel.

As Darcy took her seat next to Jenna, she breathed a sigh of relief. The meeting's guest speaker was going to give an update on the plans for the new Marysburg Library. The current facility was a hundred-year-old Carnegie-style building that was woefully out of date on the tech end. Jenna was a big supporter of the library.

Since it mattered to her, it mattered to Darcy. She even gave the speaker her full attention as she dined. That was a switch from her usual move of merely pretending to pay attention.

When the presentation was finished, the organization's president worked his way through the rest of the day's agenda at a rapid pace. Darcy's hopes rose that they might be out of there before one o'clock.

Those hopes were dashed when the floor was opened for general discussion. Todd Meadows raised his hand. He exchanged a smirk with the woman seated next to him, art dealer Jasmine Longoria. In recent months, their under-the-radar affair had become official. Todd was now in the process of divorcing his current wife. One time, Darcy told Jenna she hoped the soon-to-be ex-wife would take Todd to the cleaners and back.

The man cleared his throat as he got to his feet. "I have a question for the police chief. Is there any progress on your murder investigation?"

The chief stood. He was an imposing man at six feet, four inches tall, with short silver hair. Though he had a thin build that always made Darcy think of Lyle Lovett, the muscle definition under his fitted shirt left no doubt he wasn't be messed with.

"First off, I'd like to thank you all for your support during this unfortunate time. As you know, I'm not at liberty to discuss specifics of the case. I can tell you we're pursuing a number of avenues of inquiry and last night uncovered a key piece of evidence."

Jenna turned to Darcy and raised her eyebrows.

"I'll tell you after the meeting," Darcy said in a whisper.

"Does that mean you know who the murderer is?" the owner of the local independent grocery store asked.

"I really can't comment on that. Investigations like this take time. Mr. Tufnell's associates have been very helpful by agreeing to stay in town while we investigate. We want to make sure we've done all we can while they're still here."

"Can't you make them stay? You know, like the 'don't leave town' thing cops say on TV?" The question was from someone in the back of the room Darcy couldn't see.

"No. That would amount to what's called false imprisonment. We've asked for, and received, contact information from each one of them. We know how to get ahold of them after they leave town, if need be."

"So that's it." Todd, still standing, crossed his arms. "They can just waltz out of here any time they, please? I heard the wife left town yesterday. Did you know about that?"

The chief shot the realtor the kind of look that would leave most people quivering in their Doc Martins. It seemed that Todd was either out to embarrass the police or simply stir up trouble. Either seemed quite possible. Regardless of the motive, he had Darcy's full attention.

"Mrs. Tufnell needed to return home so she could be with her family and begin funeral arrangements. We had absolutely no objection to letting the

146

wife of the deceased do that. Do you have a point, Mr. Meadows?"

"Yes. As a matter of fact, I do." He straightened the knot of his tie and focused his attention on the crowd. "The Marysburg Center is a wonderful facility that has served its residents well. I don't think it's in the community's best interest for it to host touring rock performances. After all, look at what happened. A murder. And if what the Chief says is accurate, it was committed by someone in the victim's inner circle. Do we want that kind of mob coming to our community ever again?"

"Now, you hold on a minute." Darcy shot to her feet. "I know I'm new to this group, but I won't keep my mouth shut while that man runs down an event that brought a lot of dollars to this community. A lot of good press, at least at first."

Murmurs of assent rumbled through the crowd. Jenna gave her hand a squeeze in support. It was common knowledge that Darcy had helped torpedo a major mixed-use development that Todd had sunk tons of time and money into. The building that housed Marysburg Music had been a critical piece of the proposed construction project. Her refusal to give in when the real estate developer tried to pry it out of her hands stopped the project from breaking ground. The support from the group, though muted, was energizing.

"Perhaps, but at what cost? How much did the city have to spend in dollar and man hours cleaning up after the event? I heard there was trash strewn for blocks and that someone was arrested for trying to break into the theater during the show." He shook his head. "That's not the kind of crowd Marysburg, Indiana wants or needs."

A few clapped in response to Todd's reply. Darcy seemed to have the support of the majority of those in attendance, though.

"Mr. Meadows' complaints are a distraction. Instead of complaining and interrogating the Chief like he's a suspect, I think we should be thanking the Chief for everything he and Detective-Sergeant Rosengarten are doing to track down the murderer." She placed her fingertips on the tabletop and stared at Todd for a moment, then looked at the police officer. "So, thank you, Chief. Keep up the good work. I also want to announce that Marysburg

Music will be holding a memorial concert Wednesday night instead of our usual open mic event. We'll be announcing more details this evening."

A round of hearty applause filled the room as she dropped into her chair. She blew out a breath and put her hand over her heart. It was hammering against her chest like she'd just played a ten-minute drum solo.

Jenna leaned close to her. "Nice work. But telling the Chief thank you, keep up the good work thing was a little over the top."

"Maybe." She stared at Meadows. He was busy typing away on his phone. "That man has it in for me. He's going to try to bring down everything Marysburg Music is associated with."

Jenna let out a little *humph*. "Let him try. I think you'd be surprised how many people will have your back."

With the faceoff over, the meeting came to a quick conclusion. As she and Jenna exited the building, a number of fellow business owners shook her hand or patted her on the back, along with providing words of encouragement.

"Welp, that pretty much clinches it." Jenna put her arm around Darcy. "Meadows may have more money than God, but you, my friend, are way more popular."

Darcy chuckled. "That is one sentence I thought I would never hear. Gotta admit, it feels good."

"Enjoy it. You earned it. I need to get back to the restaurant. Stop by for breakfast tomorrow morning. It's on me as a little thank you for putting Mr. Moneybags in his place."

"Thanks. Talk to you then. In the meantime, I have a concert to plan."

The idea for some sort of memorial gathering had been rattling around in the back of Darcy's mind for a few days. Sure, folks had gathered at the store the day after Derek died. That had been to mourn his loss, though. She wanted to do something to celebrate the man's music.

And maybe, in the process, put pressure on the murderer.

On the walk back to work, she stopped at the Comic Castle. There was a new version of a *Sandman* graphic novel that had her name on it. Since she'd finished her book the night before, the escape from reality the book would provide would come in handy right away.

The electronic *ding dong* when she entered caught the attention of two people who were huddled over a comic. One of them was the short, roundish man known to one and all in town as the Hobbit, more formally known as Sean O'Sullivan. He nodded when Darcy waved at him.

She had a fraught relationship with the store owner, who also owned the Magic Box, the business next door that specialized in card, board, and role-playing games. Their difficulties weren't Darcy's fault.

Sure, she'd accused him of murdering her boss. In the end, there'd been good reason for her to do so. Besides, she'd gone to great lengths to keep the accusation between the two of them. If she hadn't leaned on the Hobbit as hard as she had, Eddie's murderer might still be free. Instead, that poor soul was behind bars.

And Darcy had made a good faith effort to make sure people knew Sean O'Sullivan had helped make that happen.

She strolled past the wall where the new comics were displayed. There were a dizzying number of them, from cheerful kids' adventures to dark horror stories. On the other side of the aisle, big cardboard boxes contained used comics of every genre, from *Superman* to *Star Trek* to an illustrated version of *Maverick*, the classic Western TV show, Manga books took up the majority of the back wall. It never ceased to amaze her how many different items the store carried.

And the Hobbit knew where everything was without hesitation. Even down to some random *Archies* comic from the early seventies.

"Looking for anything, in particular, Gaughan?" the Hobbit asked.

She showed him the *Sandman* graphic novel she'd been after. "Got it already. Just checking to see if you've got anything else I can't live without."

"Got a new *Josie and the Pussy Cats* that might interest you. You know, with your old job and all that." He pointed to where the item was.

"Good one. I'll have to check it out." Her perusal of the comic was interrupted by the Hobbit's animated voice as he described the plot of a *Batman* comic to the other man.

"It's amazing. Catwoman and the Riddler team up. They kidnap Robin and tie him to the top of the tallest building in Gotham City. Nobody knows where he is. At the same time, they plant a dirty bomb across town and tell the Caped Crusader he can only save one, the city or the Boy Wonder."

Darcy stopped her perusal mid-page. Something the Hobbit said had kick-started her brain, like when someone pressed the play button on a CD player. She double-timed it over to the two men.

"What did you just say?"

He looked up at her, distrust in his eyes. "What do you mean? I was just telling him about—"

"I know. Sorry." She stepped back and took a breath. "The comic, who's the bad guy?"

"Not bad guy, bad guys, or villains, to be accurate. Catwoman and the Riddler. They don't team up as often as I'd like. That's what…."

The rest of his explanation was lost on Darcy. Her brain went into overdrive, this time like pressing the fast-forward button on a cassette player. Two bad guys. Two people plotting together to take down the hero. It made perfect sense.

What if two people had worked together to murder Derek?

"Sean, you are a genius." She shoved the graphic novel and comic in his hands. "I'll take these and all the *Josie and the Pussycats* comics you have."

The store owner looked around. "What's going on? Am I on some kind of new version of *Candid Camera*?"

"Nope." She practically floated to the sales counter. "Something way better. You may have just helped solve Derek Tufnell's murder."

Chapter Twenty

"Let me get this straight." Liam tossed a stick into the water. He was quiet until the ripples it created were swept away by the flow of Mary's Creek as it made the juncture with the White River. "You think not one, but two, people murdered Derek? Seriously?"

"Yep." Darcy handed him a bison burger hot off the hibachi. They were enjoying an evening cooking out on the deck. The opportunity to pass the time outdoors was running short, with the cold rains of November not far off.

"I thought the coroner's report already ruled that out. That he was dead by the time he was hit on the head."

She placed a plate with tiny bison scraps in front of Ringo. She'd been gone so much more than normal, the feline deserved to partake in their feast, too.

"That's true." She rubbed her forehead to force herself to slow down, then plopped a serving of potato salad on both of their plates. "The poison killed him. The more I think about it, the more convinced I am that two people in Derek's circle worked together to take him out. Camron Jessup may have some issues, but he's not a murderer."

Liam bit into his burger. He let out a little moan and wiped his chin as he chewed. "God, this is good. You think Jessup was set up to be the patsy by the killers, then. Right?"

She nodded as she got settled in the chair next to Liam. "That makes the most sense to me. The way I figure things, it was way too complicated for one person to pull off poisoning Derek by spiking the water."

"Why not?" He wiped his chin again. "People were busy setting up. Derek was at the record store for a while. Then there was the sound check. Do you have everyone's whereabouts accounted for the whole time?"

"No. But hear me out. For one person to do it, they would have had to get their hands on the bottles of water. Then they would have needed someplace to spike the bottles. Then they would have to make sure the bottles got taken inside and put in the fridge in the green room. And then make sure he drank it. That's a tall order for one person, don't you think?"

"That is a lot. I'll grant you that." He took another bite of his burger. A chilly breeze coming from across the water blew his hair into his eyes for a moment. Darcy would have made a suggestive comment about it if they didn't have heavier issues to deal with.

"Let's start at the beginning. Where'd the bottled water come from?"

"I don't know." Darcy pulled on a Marysburg Music hoodie. Even though it was only seven o'clock, the sun had already set and taken its warming glow with it. "It's a fancy brand of flavored water. If I remember right, it had three lions on it the label. Chris said the contract required it. He didn't want to screw around with purchasing it, so they agreed the tour would provide it, and he'd pay them back."

Liam was working on his phone as Darcy talked. "Yep, here we go. It's from England. The three lions tipped me off."

"I assume you knew that from your Premier League weekends?" Liam had recently become obsessed with English football. You could depend on him being in front of his TV for a match weekend mornings when he wasn't working.

"Score one for the American detective." He put up his hand for a high five. "So, it's an exclusive brand. The closest place you might be able to get it is Indy, or more likely, Chicago."

Darcy tossed a morsel of her bison burger to Ringo as she got to her feet to pace the deck.

"This tour was supposed to go to a lot of smaller places like this so he could personally apologize to the women he took advantage of. It makes sense that they'd buy the water in bulk whenever they could get it and bring it along with them. I mean, it's not like it was going to go bad."

"In that case, it sounds to me like pretty much everyone on the tour bus would have access to it."

"Yes, one hundred percent. Another reason for it most likely being an inside job. How about this? Brian supposedly came to town as a show of support for Derek. While he wasn't traveling with the rest of the group, he would have been able to get his hands on the water, too."

"When?"

It was a simple enough question. It was a key one, too.

"While the band was setting up. They only had two techs with them. The musicians would have had to help with setup. Except for Derek."

"Okay, say you're right, and Brian poisoned the water while everyone else was busy. Where does your second person come in?"

"The second person made sure Derek kept drinking the poisoned water. They were probably all like, 'You need to keep your fluids up. Don't want to get dehydrated during your first show.' Something along that line."

"Who would have done that?" One of the things Darcy adored about Liam was that he didn't overthink things. He was an expert at getting right to the point.

"Vanessa makes the most sense to me. How does this sound? Brian shows up while everyone is unloading. He poisons the water while they're too busy to notice what he's doing and slips away. Then, he gives Vanessa some kind of sign. She fetches the water and puts it in the cooler in the green room. What do you think, Ringo?"

The cat got up on all fours, blinked at her, then sauntered toward the house.

"See? He thinks it's case closed."

Liam laughed. He got up and made himself another burger. "Don't want to let these get cold."

"You think I'm on the right track, then." It wasn't a question. Darcy fully expected Liam to agree with her.

"To borrow some of your crime-fighting lingo, it checks the Means and Opportunity boxes. I get it that Brian was popping off about Derek being worth more dead than alive. What's the motive for Vanessa, though?"

Darcy stared up at the sky. A few stars were out, shining bright against the vast blackness of Space. As lovely as the celestial bodies were, they had no help to give her. Liam's question had her stumped.

"I don't know. She seemed so excited about the tour. There were all these grand plans to move to larger venues after the first of the year."

"Doesn't sound like a murderer to me."

"Unless Brian was holding something over her head. Or she was lying." Darcy put the remaining burger patty on a plate. She'd have it for lunch sometime later. Then she poured water over the coals. She was self-aware enough to recognize her actions as delay tactics.

She knew all too well about lying. Once she started losing control during the Pixie Dust days, lying to herself had become easy. One more drink wouldn't affect her playing. Her elbow wasn't hurting. The band couldn't survive without her.

All lies.

While she'd gotten better at spotting her own lies, she'd also become pretty adept at seeing through the lies of others. Like how Vanessa always seemed to shove her hands into her pockets when probing questions were asked. It was a sign of guilt. Yes, now that Darcy had time to think things over, she was certain.

The tour manager was lying.

"What would she be lying about, Darc?" Liam joined her by the hibachi. "She's a tour manager, right? I mean, isn't it their job to keep the tour on track? Why would she want to put herself out of work?"

Stirring the coals calmed her. It allowed her mind to slow down. To let the answer come to her. When it did, she made a fist pump.

"Why would she put herself out of work, my friend? Because Brian gave her an offer she couldn't refuse. He used whatever information he had on her and made her do it."

The night had become still. The only sound was the rustling of the leaves that hadn't fallen. Even the creek had taken a break from its usual ebb and flow.

Then Liam let out a breath.

"I think that sounds a little overdramatic. Don't you?"

She glared at him for a moment. Then punched him in the arm. "I don't need you in my life. I have a cat."

He rubbed his arm. "I may have to apply for disability after that punch. I need that arm for work."

Despite her best efforts, she couldn't keep from grinning. "You are such a wimp. Will it help if I kiss it?"

"It would help more if you kissed this." He pointed to his cheek. "And then these." He pointed to his lips.

"Holy smokes, you are such a dork. But since you asked nicely." She pressed her lips to his cheek, then a quick peck on the lips.

"Better?"

"Much." He kissed her back. "Interested in taking this discussion inside?"

Butterflies danced around inside Darcy. Though welcome, it was still a strange sensation. One she wasn't certain how to respond to. Liam was trustworthy, though. She slipped her hand into his.

"Works for me. But be forewarned. Ringo won't put up with any funny business."

"I promise to be a gentleman."

"Excellent. If you're not too much of a gentleman, that might be okay. Just saying."

Chapter Twenty-One

Hanging out with Liam had proven to be just what Darcy needed. In more ways than one. Having her day off come on the heels of his visit was a bonus. That meant she got to sleep in.

At least as late as Ringo would allow.

The feline roused her from a deep sleep a little after eight o'clock.

"Come on, dude. It's my day to chill."

He stared at her without blinking for a full minute. When she didn't move, he rubbed his cheek against her hand, then climbed down the small set of steps from the bed to the floor.

The poor guy had been showing his age and couldn't make the leap from the floor to the bed any longer. The veterinarian had diagnosed him with a touch of arthritis in his hips. He was basically fine but wasn't able to make high jumps anymore.

The solution was to install a few sets of "stairs" for him. With them in place, he was able to get up on the bed as well as his favorite window perch. Whenever Darcy saw him use the stairs, she got the warm fuzzies inside. It was a great feeling.

That didn't change the fact she wasn't ready to get out of bed.

"All right, fine." With a grumble, she threw back the covers. In Ringo's defense, her alarm normally went off at seven, so he had allowed her to sleep in for an hour. Sometimes, his feline generosity knew no bounds.

My, how times had changed. Every now and then, it seemed like only yesterday that she was touring with Pixie Dust, staying up until three A.M. and not getting out of bed until noon or later when they arrived at the next tour stop.

As Darcy showered, after feeding Ringo, of course, she replayed the previous evening's conversation with Liam. The glamorous life of the touring musician was a big fat lie most of the time. In reality, it was a grind.

Play a gig. Get on the tour bus if you were a big enough act to afford that luxury. If not, squeeze into a van and try to get some sleep. Arrive at the next town. Try to get in a little exercise. Conduct a sound check. Play the gig. Do it all over again.

For weeks or months at a time.

The rare days off between gigs were more precious than all the platinum records in the world. That's when you did glamorous things like the laundry, get groceries so you weren't subsisting on takeout, and try to rest and recharge.

You didn't get paid on days off, though, so you tried to limit them to no more than one or two per week.

Back in the day, Darcy had loved every minute of it.

Of course, back in the day, she thought she was going to live forever, bulletproof, indestructible. You name it.

These days, Darcy recognized that behavior as the Burn The Candle At Both Ends lifestyle of Youth. All things considered, she wouldn't trade her past with anyone. Was youth wasted on the young? That was for deeper thinkers to decide. What she knew was that the current version of Darcy Gaughan was the sum of her experiences. All the good mixed right in with all the bad.

Those experiences were proving to be majorly helpful with her investigation. Thank goodness for small favors.

While she munched on a breakfast of granola and yogurt, she texted Paul asking if they'd recovered any fingerprints from Sunday evening's discovery.

It took a while, but he eventually responded no. On the upside, they were able to recover trace amounts of antifreeze from the jug. They were awaiting testing results to find out if it contained the same lethal ingredient that killed Derek.

He followed up with another text a few moments later. Both the Chief and

Detective-Sergeant Rosengarten had praised him for his initiative. Darcy's name had not been brought up in any way, shape, or fashion. He owed her one.

She let out a sigh of relief. No official involvement was good.

The lack of fingerprints bummed her out, though. Finding even a single fingerprint could have led the police straight to the murderer. Case solved. Assuming the murderer had been fingerprinted by law enforcement in the past, of course.

Then an idea popped into her head. She sent off another text.

No prints at all? Like not even from some rando who put it on a store shelf?

The response was as short as it had been swift. *No. Working on locating purchase point*

"Okay, Ringo. That's less than ideal. It'll take a while for the cops to figure out where the antifreeze was bought. Then, even if they can do that, they'll need to figure out who purchased it. That's going to take time. Too much of it."

The cat let out a sad-sounding *mrrr*.

"I know, buddy. It's not all doom and gloom, though. With no fingerprints at all, that shows the murderer took the time to wipe the whole thing down. Just like the award was wiped clean. Coincidence?"

The old tomcat paused long enough from drinking at his water fountain to glance at her. He ran his tongue around his mouth, making sure to catch every water droplet.

That was encouragement for Darcy. "Agreed, buddy. Cops aren't supposed to believe in coincidence. We won't either."

So, the jug containing the antifreeze used to murder Derek and the award that was used to look like a murder weapon were both devoid of fingerprints. What did that mean? She ran her spoon around the edge of the bowl to capture the remaining granola. She shook her head. Asking what it meant was the wrong question.

The right question was to ask what did it prove? The answer to that, for the moment at least, was not much.

The murderer, or murderers, were thorough. Beyond that, she was drawing a blank.

That was okay. Her conversation with Liam had left her with more than one avenue of investigation. She dialed a number.

"Hey, Chris. Do you mind if I swing by to ask a few more questions about the day of the concert?"

The man's office was on the second floor of the theater building. He was seated behind a desk which wasn't much more than a pressboard platform with metal supports at either end. A crank handle extended from the support at one end of the desk. It was one of those adjustable models which let the user work sitting or standing.

Char often spoke fondly about the one she had back in her accounting days. They could get expensive. The luxury item seemed out of place compared to the rest of the office. Then again, Chris put a lot of time in the room. It wasn't Darcy's place to judge.

He looked up from his computer screen when she knocked on the door frame.

"Grab a seat." He gestured toward a pair of folded-up director's chairs that were leaning against a wall. "Just need to finish this email."

Rather than sitting, she gazed at the collection of framed posters on one wall. A *School of Rock* poster was flanked by ones for *The Lion, The Witch, and The Wardrobe* and *The Music* Man. It took her a second to recognize the significance. They were posters for shows the Civic Theater group had put on.

"What's up?"

Chris' question interrupted her, marveling at a stunning poster of *Wicked*. She tapped her finger on the frame's glass.

"That's my favorite musical ever." She grabbed one of the directors' chairs, leaning against a wall, and sat.

"Is that so? I figured you for an *American Idiot* kind of gal."

She smiled. "That's a great album, but I've never seen the stage adaptation. I guess I really identify with Elphaba's story. Someone who's misunderstood resonates with me."

"Yeah, I'd imagine so." He rubbed his hands together. "You didn't come to talk poster art. How can I be of service?"

"I'd like to go over a few points about the day of the show."

"No problem. I've replayed that day in my head so many times by now, I feel like I could write a book about it. Whatever I can do to help."

"Great." She brought him up to speed on the highlights of the investigation. "When we talked last time, you told me about the deal with Derek being all picky about his water."

"Don't forget the flavored part."

"Right. Do you know where the water came from? Was it delivered, or did Derek's group already have it?"

He scratched his chin, then nodded. "Okay, yeah. The tour bus had arrived. The band and their technicians were unloading equipment. While they were doing that, I was talking with the tour manager about where to put up a station for merch sales."

"Go on." So far, his report made sense. Merch sales were an important stream of revenue for a touring operation. As the tour manager, Vanessa would have wanted to make sure the merch table was in a location concert-goers couldn't miss. Based on Thea's haul, the choice of location had been a good one.

"I was showing the woman some options when the producer guy, Paul, came in. He told us he'd brought the water in and had left it at the concession stand."

"Do you remember where he said he brought it from? This is super important."

"Not that I remember. He said something like, 'Tonight's water allotment for Derek is on the counter. You should get it refrigerated as soon as possible. He likes it chilled.'"

The information wasn't as valuable as a hit record, but it was helpful. It confirmed Paul had possession of the water. Even though it was for an unspecified amount of time, there could be no dispute he had laid hands on it. It also confirmed he was the one who brought it indoors.

"This is super helpful, Chris. Now, do you know who took the water back to the dressing room?"

"Yeah." This time there was no hesitation in his answer. "When Vanessa and I agreed on the location for the merch table, she went to get it. I remember I went over to the soundboard and saw her head backstage with it."

The facts were lining up with Darcy's theory. A thrill ran through her at the thought that she had Derek's murderers in sight.

"Were the bottles in plastic wrap or something like what you see at the grocery store?"

"No. She was carrying them in a six-pack caddy. The reusable kind people use when they buy craft beer singles at the store." He chewed on his lip for a moment. "Is any of this really helpful? The cops already asked me pretty much the same questions."

"It is, trust me. So much so, the next time we're both at Selena's, I've got your dinner and drinks tab."

"Tell you what, you spring for a PBR for me, we'll call it even. I don't go for that fancy microbrew stuff."

"You've got yourself a deal." She shook his hand to seal the arrangement.

"Excellent. Any chance that means you know who the killer is?" The hope in his eyes was heartbreaking. He'd done absolutely nothing wrong throughout this affair. Yet, the guilt he carried was clear for anyone to see.

If she could absolve him of that guilt, Darcy would. In a heartbeat. She had to be honest with him, though. It would be unfair, cruel even, to give him false hope.

"I don't. I'm getting close, though. Really close."

Chapter Twenty-Two

Darcy had a couple of more stops to make, but before she could do that, she needed to follow up on the plans for the memorial concert she'd thrown together. The reception to the announcement on social media had been so positive she'd gotten teary-eyed. Now, all she had to do was come up with performers. Thank goodness she knew her fair share of musicians.

When Darcy sprung the idea on them at the store the day before, Izzy and Peter had agreed to perform on one condition. Darcy had to play drums with them.

"We can do a jazz trio thing," Izzy had said. "Me on sax, Pete on bass, and you drums."

"It'll be perfect, Boss. Yesi." Peter had put his hands together, as if I prayer. "I can play some of the music for my audition, too."

"Fine, but you know my elbow's only good for a half hour tops." Darcy massaged it for good measure.

In response, the kids had promised to see if they could get any other members of the high school's jazz ensemble to play. A group of high school kids, who were massively talented, it had to be said, and a has-been punk rocker was hardly the kind of lineup Darcy had in mind.

Which was why she made the Marysburg House her next stop.

She found Gwen first. Her fellow drummer was reading a book on the front porch. "Mind if I join you?"

"Be my guest." She closed the paperback. It was Malcolm Gladwell's *Outliers*.

"Heady stuff." Darcy raised her eyebrows. She loved the escape her mysteries and the occasional thriller provided.

"I was bored out of my skull, and this was on the bookshelf. I'd heard about it, so I figured, why not give it a try."

"And?"

"Jury's still out. No doubt that the guy's super smart. Don't know that I'm ready to buy his premise yet."

"Fair enough." Darcy drummed her fingers on her thigh. She'd been practicing her pitch, but all of a sudden, it sounded silly. Well, too late now. "Are you still going to be in town tomorrow night?"

"Yeah. The cops told us all yesterday they found some new evidence. We took a vote and agreed to hang until the end of the week in case they have a breakthrough. Why?"

"I'm putting together a little memorial concert for Derek at my record store tomorrow evening. I thought I'd ask you and the rest of the band members if you'd like to come. And maybe even sit in on a song or two."

Gwen's silence was unnerving. It had been a gamble approaching the woman Derek had harassed. She was the one Darcy'd established the most rapport with, though.

"If you'd rather not, I totally get it."

The woman nodded, then cracked a smile. "I remember listening to Pixie Dust in my bedroom and air drumming along. Back then, my number one goal in life was to meet you. The thought of playing drums alongside you was too big of a dream to even consider."

Darcy's cheeks got hot. She'd been on the receiving end of a lot of kind words and compliments in recent years. Those had been due to her efforts to remain sober and her work at the record store. It had been ages since someone spoke of her work in Pixie Dust with such affection.

"Thank you." She wiped a tear from the corner of her eye. "That's really kind of you. I appreciate it."

"So, this show of yours. Is it Derek Tufnell music only, or can artists play what they want?"

"Derek's music would be amazing, but you can play whatever you want.

163

I'm sitting in with a couple of local jazz musicians. We're going to do some Mindy Abair and Charles Mingus."

"That's cool. I'm in. On one condition."

Darcy's heart skipped a beat. "Sure. Anything."

"You do a couple of Dust songs with me."

"Oh." She took a moment. Nobody had asked her to play Pixie Dust in ages. Could she still do it? She'd never know unless she tried. "I think that can be arranged."

They discussed details for a few moments. Darcy would have Peter pick up Gwen and her electronic drum kit the following afternoon. On the way to the store, Gwen would give Peter the music he'd need for his part of the two Pixie Dust songs they were going to perform. In the meantime, Darcy would do some exercises so she could handle vocals.

"Do we need a guitarist? I can set something up at the store so we can play with an audio track if that would be easier." All of a sudden, Darcy was excited about playing her old music. She hadn't felt this way in ages.

"I'll get Drew to do it. He's been as bored as me." She twirled her fingers with imaginary drumsticks. "I'll mention it to Hambone, too. If he tries to come up with an excuse, I'll put a guilt trip on him. Nothing ventured, nothing gained, right?"

Darcy let out a long laugh. "You are so right, sister."

Gwen told Darcy that Vanessa had been last seen practicing yoga in the back yard. She found the tour manager in a cool-down position. When the woman was finished with her corpse pose, Darcy offered her a towel that had been draped over a wrought iron chair nearby.

"Good workout?"

Vanessa accepted it with a smile. "Yeah. I'm from So Cal, so I got my start doing yoga on the beach. As long as I'm outside, I'll do a session. Unless it's cold out."

"This isn't too cold for you?" Darcy looked down at her attire of blue jeans and a purple fleece.

"I was a little chilly at the start. That didn't last." She took a drink from a plastic water bottle. "What brings you by?"

CHAPTER TWENTY-TWO

"A couple of things. Do you have a minute?"

Vanessa sat in one of the wrought iron chairs. She motioned for Darcy to join her.

"Every Wednesday and Saturday, the record store has open mic night. Tomorrow, the we're hosting a memorial concert for Derek. It's nothing fancy. Some local musicians getting together to make some music, but it's an important event for the community. Gwen's going to join us. She's going to see if Drew and Hambone will, too. I wanted to invite you, too."

"Oh, wow. Between you and me, I was planning on going home tomorrow. We've given the police enough time to solve this."

"I totally understand." That was a lie. Darcy didn't understand why Vanessa was so ready to leave town when the group had supposedly given the police until Friday before leaving. "Any chance I can talk you into staying one more night? Gwen and I are going to play some Pixie Dust. If nothing else, it'll be a cringeworthy moment to put on YouTube and other socials. There's no such thing as bad publicity. Know what I mean?"

"I'll think about it. You said you had two things you wanted to talk to me about?"

"Yeah." This was going to take a much more delicate touch, especially if Vanessa was Brian's partner in murder. "I guess I'm looking for someone to vent with. I can't believe Derek's bottles of water were messed with. I've been on a tour bus, just like the rest of you all. I've been wracking my mind, and I can't see where someone would have the chance to do that. You know as well as I do there are no secrets on the bus. How could the murderer have gotten to them?"

For a moment, the woman stiffened. Then she took a drink of water.

"I know what you mean. We keep, kept, a supply in a cargo bay to make sure Derek had his water when we visited small towns like this. There were three bottles in the fridge. The cops took those. They hadn't been tampered with."

"What about the rest?"

"We left Boston with four cases worth, ninety-six, in all. After the six bottles Derek drank the day of the show and the ones in the fridge, that left eighty-seven. The cops took it all. Every bottle was accounted for. As far as I know, the six he drank that day were the only ones tampered with."

Vanessa seemed to know quite a bit about the investigation. Then again, she was the tour manager. It would make sense that she'd be the group's point person with the police.

"Sounds like the murderer knew the exact amount they wanted to poison."

"Yeah. That's why I can't stay here any longer. It's too hard to look at those people knowing one of them murdered Derek."

It was a convincing performance, so far. Now it was time to see if Vanessa could stick the landing.

"Any idea where the tainted bottles came from?"

"I thought I did, but I can't be certain anymore." She rubbed her forehead with her thumb and index finger. "All I know is that six bottles were waiting at the concession stand when I finished talking to the theater manager about a few things. I assumed one of the techs had brought them in when we were unloading."

Interesting. She could have totally thrown Brian to the wolves at that moment. Why didn't she? Instead, she was doing a credible job of making herself out as an innocent victim in the whole affair. Darcy wanted to tip her hat to the woman. If it wasn't for the fact that she'd just lied through her teeth.

"Had Paul arrived by then? Maybe he brought them in."

"That would be just like him. Doing something halfway." She seemed to catch herself. "No. Now that I think about it, I think he did drop them off at the concession stand. I don't know how long they were there, though. Like I said, I was busy with the theater manager."

Good save, girl. She'd verified what Chris had said while leaving enough of a hole to plant a seed of doubt implying someone else had tampered with the bottles while they were at the concession stand.

Darcy gave Vanessa's elbow a friendly squeeze. "I am so, so sorry all of you are going through this. I appreciate you letting me vent. I don't think the cops appreciate how tough this is on all of you, what with you all being far away from home."

"At least you understand." She looked around. "You'll keep this conversation between the two of us, right? I don't want anyone to think I'm throwing someone under the bus. Sorry about that. Poor choice of words. I was the tour manager. It was my responsibility to keep everyone safe. And I failed."

Darcy got down on one knee and looked Vanessa in the eye. "Listen to me. You did not fail. Preventing a murder is not in any tour manager's job description. Don't worry. I'm sure the murderer will be behind bars, and this will be over soon enough."

"Thank you."

"You take care of yourself." Darcy stood. "By the way, do you know if Paul's around? I want to invite him to the show tomorrow night, too."

"I, uh, don't know. You might check inside."

Darcy gave Vanessa another word of encouragement, then headed for the house. She needed to talk to Paul before Vanessa tipped him off.

She ran into Hambone in the foyer. He raised his leather cowboy hat to her.

"Good to see you again, Darcy. Gwen just told me about the little jam session you've got tomorrow night. If you got room for a set of keyboards, I'll be there."

Her heart swelled, and her vision got cloudy. Here was Derek's oldest friend, his long-time collaborator, committing to the event. An event borne out of a desperate ploy to prove Todd Meadows wrong. That the rock and roll community was a kind and caring community.

A community not unlike Marysburg Music.

"Thank you so much. You don't know how much your presence will mean to everyone. You worked with Derek longer than I've been alive."

The grin he'd been sporting faltered at the final comment. "Come on now. You're going to make me feel old. Don't get me wrong. I know I am. I just don't want to feel like it."

"Sorry about that. Sometimes my mouth gets ahead of my brain."

"No harm done." The grin returned. "I've heard you're poking around into my buddy's murder. Trying to outwit the Man?"

She gave him a nervous chuckle. One of her feet was already in her mouth.

Inserting the other would be awful with a capital A.

"Nothing like that. Even though it's been a while, I remember how life on the road is. Derek was murdered in my community. I kind of owe it to him and my town to put whatever insight I may have to good use."

"That's admirable of you. I'm sure Derek would appreciate it."

"Along that line, you knew him better than anyone. Who do you think would want to harm him?"

The man tilted his head to the right, as if appraising her. Trying to determine if she was trustworthy, perhaps. In response to the lengthy gaze, Darcy broke out in goosebumps. He put his hand on her shoulder.

"I can't say who murdered him. What I can tell you is that the walls in this place aren't as thick as some people would like them to be."

"What do you mean?"

"My room's next door to Vanessa's. Let's just say a few times she's had a late-night visitor. She's not a quiet one, if you get my drift." He winked.

The lecherous picture he drew made Darcy's skin crawl. What two consenting adults did behind doors was their own business.

A man was dead, though. If an affair was connected to the murder, Darcy was obligated to look into it.

"Who's the visitor?" She hated herself for asking the question. Sometimes, searching for the truth was the worst.

"Our esteemed producer. Makes me wonder what else they may be up to behind everyone's backs. Like murdering my friend, maybe?"

"Why?" Money was the logical answer. She wanted Hambone to either confirm that assumption or give her another thread to follow. After all, his mysterious phone call hadn't been forgotten.

"What else? Money. Brian swears he promised Derek he wouldn't record the concert since it was the first show of the tour, but I know better. He'll make a mint on a live album. Then he'll connect his little lady with a band playing arenas. A lot more money there for her. It's a win-win for the both of them."

Hambone's explanation made all the sense in the world. Something didn't sound quite right, though. Like a song that was missing a key percussion track. It came to her just in time.

"I'll keep an eye on them. By the way, do you know who owns the rights to Derek's music? There will be a lot of money in that, too."

"I wish I did. I can't tell you that, either, I'm afraid. See you tomorrow night." He tipped his hat to her again and strolled toward the door.

"Looking forward to it." Especially because she was pretty sure Hambone had lied to her every bit as much as Vanessa had. What, specifically, he had lied about, she wasn't certain.

That begged the question. What was he hiding? Darcy decided at that moment that she was giving herself twenty-four to find out.

The murderer would be revealed at the memorial jam session. She was going to make sure of it.

Chapter Twenty-Three

Darcy lingered in the Marysburg House's foyer, mulling over her next move. Or, more to the point, the ethics thereof. She wasn't above playing dumb to get information out of someone. But straight out lying to a suspect seemed awfully underhanded.

This was murder, though. The worst of all crimes. She'd debate the moral implications of her behavior with Ringo and Liam at a later date.

She dashed up the stairs, taking them two at a time. The luxurious carpeting muffled her footfalls. That would come in handy if she was going to take Brian by surprise.

The landing at the top of the stairs opened up to a wide hallway with three rooms on either side. Another set of stairs led up to the third floor. If memory served, the two bedrooms on that level were smaller than the ones on the second floor, so they'd probably been given to the crew.

Brian had to be behind one of the doors on this floor. With no other stealthy options in mind, she decided to figure it out the old-fashioned way.

She'd listen at the door.

Light snoring came from one of the rooms on the left. Darcy decided that was Drew's room since she hadn't seen him. A man's voice, though muffled, could be heard coming from the room at the end of the hall on the right.

She tip-toed to it, then placed her ear against the old-fashioned keyhole to listen.

"That's correct. I want a portion of all profits from his date of death going forward to be earmarked for charity." There was a pause, like he was listening to someone on the other end of a call. Eavesdropping and only getting half of a conversation was proving to be quite frustrating. "We'll figure out which charities later. The point is, we need to get this announcement out now, before any bad press has a chance to kill sales momentum. We've lost enough time already."

Bad press? Kill sales momentum? That caught Darcy's attention.

There were a few grunts of apparent assent before Brian returned to giving orders.

"I want it to apply to the entire catalog. It's your job to talk Barclay into it. He and I aren't exactly on speaking terms right now." More silence. "We're both suspects in a murder investigation. That's why."

Could the Barclay Paul mentioned be the one and only Hamilton "Hambone" Barclay? What would he have to be talked into? The answer wasn't revealed because Brian ended the call.

With a break in the action, she knocked. "Brian, it's me. Vanessa."

In the span of a heartbeat, he opened the door. "Hey, babe. What's...you're not Vanessa."

"Afraid not." Darcy held out her arm to keep the door open as she entered the room. She conducted a quick survey of the surroundings before she dropped into a chair by a window. "I do, however, have a few questions about her. And you."

He left the door open. "I'm going to count to three. If you're still here when I get there, I'm calling the police."

"Where did you get Derek's flavored water from?"

"What are you talking about? I'm warning you. One."

Instead of leaving, she crossed her legs. "According to two witnesses, you dropped a six-pack of it off at the concert hall's concession stand. It's not complicated. Where did you get it? What was your location when you took possession of those bottles?"

"I don't remember. Besides, I've already spoken to the police about this." He pointed toward the hall. "You need to go. Now. Two."

"This chair is pretty comfortable. I think I'll enjoy it for a bit. Plenty of time for you to speak to me about the bottles of water. Did you also tell the police you're having an affair with Vanessa? I'm sure they'd find that interesting."

He stopped looking at her long enough to shut the door. "Are you threatening me?"

"No." She took a moment to examine her nails. They would need to be trimmed before the jam session. "I'm trying to catch Derek's murderer. You remember him, right? Your longtime client? The one you said was worth more dead than alive? Whose best days were behind him? Ring any bells?"

The blood drained from his face as he crumpled right in front of her. He dropped onto the bed with a thud.

"I should never have said those things. I thought they were true until I saw him perform. I was wrong."

"At least you're being honest about that." She leaned forward, placing her elbows on her knees. "Here are the facts, Brian. You brought the water into the theater. Vanessa took it to Derek's dressing room. Later that night, you were witnessed spouting off about how Derek's worth more to you dead than alive. And then you took off halfway through the concert for a roll in the hay with someone. Despite the fact that you and Vanessa have a thing. At least you made it back in time to hang around after the show. I'm kind of amazed the cops haven't arrested you for the crime of stupidity yet."

"I didn't kill him. For all I know, someone switched the water after I dropped it off. You have to believe me."

"No, I don't. I think you poisoned the water. A dead Derek would do more for sales than a Derek who was mounting a comeback. Then you needed to find someone to help you carry out your little plot. Vanessa was the perfect choice."

"No, you've got it all wrong. I left early because I let something else do the thinking instead of my brain. The woman I was with wanted to see the tour bus. One thing led to another, and...."

"Let me guess. You don't have a name for this woman. That's awfully convenient."

"I'm telling you, I had nothing to do with his murder. What do I have to do to convince you?"

"Tell me how you came into possession of the poisoned water. The water that you carried into the theater."

He rubbed his cheeks with his hands. Darcy remembered that move from her rehab days. Paul was panicking.

"Here's what I remember. I arrived as the band was unloading. Like I said before, I was there to see how Derek looked and sounded. That's one hundred percent true. Anyway, there was a lot of the usual hustle and bustle involved with moving the equipment, supplies, merch, and all that."

"The water?"

"Right. I went up to say hi to the band and crew. Hambone had a keyboard case under one arm. He pointed into the cargo bay where the water was stored. There was a six-pack sitting by the edge of the bay opening. Hambone asked me to make sure it got into a refrigerator."

"And did you?"

"I already told you I didn't. I'd never been to the venue before and didn't feel like wandering around until I could find the green room. That's why I left it where I did. When I saw Vanessa, I figured she'd know where to take it."

The implication of Hambone was a new wrinkle. Brian hadn't proven himself to be trustworthy, though, so he could be lying about that part of his story.

Darcy made a mental note to ask the keyboard player about it. Right now, issues like the affair and future music sales were distractions. Important, but still subordinate to murder.

Maybe the distractions were on purpose. She needed to do a little pondering on that topic.

"Thank you for being straight with me. Eventually. One more thing. Derek didn't own the rights to his music from the early days. How much would you say that part of Derek's catalog is worth now?"

The man blinked, apparently not expecting such a sudden change in topic. "In today's market?" He mumbled as he did some math in his head. "Probably twenty million."

That's a lot of money. Do you know who owns it?"

"I think Hambone does. Derek got himself tied up in a few bad investment deals and ended up way in debt. Ham bailed him out. In return, Derek signed those rights over. It was pretty substantial debt at the time."

"Any idea how much?"

"A couple million."

A hunch was coming together in Darcy's head. It was too early in the process to know for sure, but it had lot of promise.

"What would you say that two million dollars would be worth in today's world?"

He shrugged. "If you assume a reasonable rate of inflation, and a steady investment return, I could see that being worth eight to ten million now."

Darcy let out a low whistle. "Taking two million dollars and turning it into something worth twenty million. That's not a bad investment."

"Why. What are you thinking?"

She headed for the door. When she put her handle on the doorknob, she turned to him. "That Hambone might have twenty million more reasons to murder Derek than you and Vanessa have."

With her mission accomplished, Darcy opened the door. Before she could step into the hall, Paul put his hand on her shoulder. "Wait."

With a spin that was faster than an old seventy-eight LP on a turntable, Darcy turned to face him. Her fists were raised. "Don't you ever touch me again without getting my permission first."

"Sorry." He stepped back. His raised hands were shaking. "What are you going to do?"

"You'll find out tomorrow night at Marysburg Music jam session we're having in Derek's honor. Be there. It will help prove your innocence."

Hambone was sitting in a rocking chair on the porch, toking away at a vape pipe. He was playing a crossword puzzle on his phone.

"Get the answers you need?" His gaze never left the screen.

"Some." She took a seat next to him. "Brian copped to the affair."

"Honesty is the best policy, after all." He smiled as he filled in a five-letter word going across.

"It's interesting you say that. He claims you gave him the poisoned water and asked him to take it inside. Is he being honest about that, too?"

The man blew out a cloud of water vapor that smelled like a campfire, or maybe pipe tobacco. "I remember saying hi to him while we were unloading. It was a hectic scene. You know how it is."

"So, did you or did you not ask him to take a six-pack of Derek's flavored water inside?"

"I can't really say. It's been a minute."

"Are you calling him a liar?"

"I'm calling him cheap. Two techs for the four of us? And one of them was the sound engineer. Derek got priority for the other one. That left the rest of us to fend for ourselves. I mean, come on. I haven't hauled my own gear since the seventies."

"You had to know that going in."

"I did. I just didn't believe Derek when he told me. He said it would be like we were starting over, getting back to our roots. I should have paid more attention to the fine print. Never figured he would do that to me."

"Sounds like it made you mad."

"Sure, but I got over it. I'm a professional.

"Well, you sure did your part in putting on a whale of a show." She didn't want to antagonize him too much. She needed him at the jam session. "Any idea what your plans are next?"

He shook his head. "I've had a lot of time to think. I don't know. Maybe I'll hang up the life on the road. Keep appearances down to special occasions. Maybe do a music festival or two during the summer."

"It's great to know you can afford to do that. I've heard you're a bit of a financial guru. Good for you."

"I've always paid attention to what's going on around me. At the end of the day, it's all been about looking out for number one. If I don't, who will? Know what I mean?"

"That I do." Darcy understood the sentiment as well as she understood the intricacies of her drum kit.

That understanding also made her wonder if looking out for number one included committing murder.

Chapter Twenty-Four

With so many facts, hints, allegations, and lies to sift through, Darcy headed for Marysburg Music. She needed time in front of the suspect board.

"Darcy, this is quite the unexpected surprise." Hank smiled, then furrowed his eyebrows. "Is anything wrong?"

A handful of customers were perusing the aisles as another was waiting for Charlotte to finish ringing up their purchase. She didn't want to alarm anybody.

"Nope. Just need to fetch something from the office." She started toward the back of the store.

Hank knew better. He caught up with her outside the office door.

"Would you like some help? After all, I believe you, Char, and I agreed you would not step inside this store on Tuesdays. You need time away." He raised an eyebrow. It was the look he gave her that indicated he knew she was up to something.

"Maybe later." She glanced toward Charlotte at the sales counter. "I'm getting close. Give me time with the board, and I'll fill both of you in."

"Then, by all means, proceed." He opened the door and gestured for her to enter. When she was at her desk, he closed it.

The support was yet another reminder of how fortunate she was to work with some of the most kind and amazing folks around.

"Okay, girl." She uncapped a blue dry-erase marker. "Time to fill in the blanks and see if I'm right about who murdered Derek."

The first thing Darcy did was erase the names of all suspects but three. It was down to Brian, Vanessa, or Hambone. Brian and Vanessa may have been working together. They may have been working separately, too.

Regardless, the duo was involved in Derek's murder. Whether it was willingly or as patsies for Hambone, the answer was there, within Darcy's grasp.

"Let's go back to the beginning." She cued up Lake Street Dive on her phone and got to work. With each piece of information she added to the timeline, the windows during which the water could be tampered with got smaller.

Thirty minutes later, her timeline was as complete as it was going to get without assistance from Marysburg PD. Which basically meant it was finished. Paul had stuck his neck out enough to get her this far. It was up to her to carry the case to the end of the show.

That didn't mean she had to do it alone, though.

"Hey, y'all." She gave her team a wave. "Got some updates."

"Derek's band members have agreed to perform at tomorrow's memorial jam session. Here's what we need to get done." She handed a task list to Charlotte. "Start with social media posting. When Izzy gets here, assign her whatever you want on the list. The store needs to look spotless."

She put her arm around Hank. "Want to do some internet research for me? It's for my special project."

"Hey," Char stuck out her bottom lip in a fake pout. "How come he gets the fun job?"

"Because, my dear General Manager, you've mentioned how much fun managing the store's social media is. I don't want to deprive you of that."

"Whatever. You know, sometimes you're full of as much b.s. as Eddie was."

"Learned from the best, my dear."

They laughed, then Darcy pulled Hank aside so the three customers in the store wouldn't overhear her. "I need you to find out everything you can about Hamilton "Hambone" Barclay. He was Derek's long-time collaborator. Whatever you think could be connected to a motive for murder."

"Do you think he's the guy?"

"It's a long shot. Covering all my bases. Pay special attention to anything about his finances." She told him about the circumstances behind Hambone's ownership of Derek's early recordings.

"While you do that, I'm going to do the same for Brian and Vanessa. The circle is shrinking."

Alone in the office again, Darcy gazed at the board. It was like trying to get the mix for the final song on an album spot on. She needed to get it right. Otherwise, the album sounded unfinished, incomplete. Records like that disappointed fans, leaving them with a bitter taste in their mouths. Pixie Dust fans had deserved nothing but the best from her.

Derek deserved the same.

And that is when she had a *Jimmy Neutron*-style brain blast.

Throughout his career, Derek had said time and time again that he wouldn't be anything without his fans. Because of that, he owed them one hundred and ten percent. That level of commitment included recording an album as much as it included performing a show or sitting for an interview.

This tour was supposed to be his way to apologize to people he'd assaulted, hurt, taken advantage of. What if the people Derek Tufnell wanted to make amends to weren't only victims of sexual harassment and assault? What if that group of people included a songwriter who'd claimed Derek had stolen his song?

From the get-go, Darcy had dismissed Cameron Jessup's claim as the delusion of a never-was songwriter. Someone who saw Derek and his music as a means for making a buck. The matter had been litigated, and Derek won. What if the court had gotten it wrong, though?

She wanted to run through the office door, shouting at the top of her lungs that she'd had a breakthrough, like in the Hi-C commercials she saw as a kid. A stunt like that would scare the customers, though. Hank wouldn't approve. And she'd have to sweet talk Liam into installing a new door for her. He'd relish every uncomfortable moment of her explanation, too.

Instead, she took a breath, opened the door, and walked with a measured gait to the sales counter.

"Got a question for y'all." For the moment, they were the only ones in the store. Thank goodness for small favors. As long as the dearth of customers didn't last long.

"What would it mean if Cameron Jessup has been telling the truth all along?"

Charlotte raised her hand. "I know this one. It would mean that Derek stole his song and would owe Jessup a chunk of change."

"True." Hank looked up from his Internet browsing. "It would also mean that he was telling the truth about the letter. That Derek actually wanted to meet with him."

Her friends wouldn't fall back on telling Darcy what she wanted to hear. They knew her too well and were acutely aware of how honesty had gotten her through her darkest hours. That made her supposition all the more encouraging.

"Excellent." She drummed her fingers on the glass countertop. "Now, why would Derek want to meet with him? And why would he want their meeting to be held quietly?"

"To confess," Char said.

Hank immediately followed up. "And to discuss some sort of arrangement. A way to make things right."

"I love you two so much." Darcy wanted to turn cartwheels but kept the notion in check. They were too far from the finish line for any celebrating yet. "Let's say our conclusions are correct. Since Derek was calling this his apology tour, it follows he'd want to apologize to Jessup, too, right?"

When they both voiced their assent, Darcy plowed on. "Let's say that at some point Derek decided he was going announce he stole the song. I think it's safe to assume he was going to do it after he reached some sort of settlement agreement with Cameron, if he could."

"Makes sense to me." Charlotte began ticking away on her phone. "From a financial standpoint, it would be to Derek's advantage to reach an agreement before the announcement. We're talking about potentially a lot of cash. Robin Thicke and Pharrell had to pay Marvin Gaye's estate a cool five mil in one case. There are a handful of others on this post I found."

"Well, if the Jessup fellow thought he might finally get the matter resolved to his satisfaction and get paid, he wouldn't want Tufnell dead." Hank crossed his arms. "I can't find anything useful on Hambone. Where does that leave us?"

"Makes Brian a stronger suspect, doesn't it?" Charlotte's phone pinged. "Hold on. I set up Google alerts on all the suspects. Check out who has a new gig?"

Darcy's interest in the post grew with every word she read. The popular Americana band Highway 1 had just announced a European arena tour starting in December. Near the end of the report, their tour manager was mentioned.

It was Vanessa Perez.

"I thought you told us she had all these big plans for Derek's tour?" Hank said.

"She did. Now that he's gone, all of a sudden Vanessa gets to manage a bigger tour. Let's not lose focus, though." Darcy went to the display of Derek's music. "Cameron's plagiarized song, 'Path to Perdition,' is on the *Dark Clouds Ahead* album. It's called 'Keep on Knockin.'"

She pulled out a copy of the album. The back side had the track list along with something way more important. The names of the writers of each song.

"Good people of Marysburg Music, if you'll excuse me, I need to make a phone call. If it pans out like I think it will, I know who murdered Derek."

Chapter Twenty-Five

The next day, anxiety filled Darcy from the tips of her hair to the balls of her feet. It wasn't enough that she had to pull off the memorial jam session. Yes, it had to be a positive experience that would put Todd Meadows and his horrible comments back in their place. That was the secondary issue on her plate.

The headliner? She had a murderer to apprehend.

First things first, though. At three o'clock, she set up her drum kit on the platform at the back of the store. It had been years, literally, since she performed in front of a live audience. She'd performed for Liam and Ringo from time to time, keeping the beat to songs on the radio. Compared to what she was going to be doing, her tiny home "concerts" didn't count.

No pressure there.

While she was tuning her snare drum, Peter arrived with Gwen and Drew in tow. The young man was talking a mile a minute to the musicians as he helped them with their gear. His excitement was infectious, rubbing off on everyone in the store, even Darcy.

"We going to be able to pull this off, Darc?" Charlotte joined her on the platform to get a look at the store's layout. They wanted a large crowd. They needed to make sure people were safe, too. It would be a balancing act.

Especially with the murder reveal sideshow she had in store.

"Man, I hope so." She wiped a bead of sweat from her brow. "Remember, business as usual until we get to the last set. I'm going to wait until then to reveal Derek's murderer."

"That'll make for some interesting posts on social media." Charlotte chuckled. It lacked conviction, though.

"Relax. Officer Gerard's going to be here. He's off duty, so he won't be in uniform to tip anyone off. He agreed to bring his cuffs, though. Just in case."

"Look at you. Working with the cops to bring down the bad guy. Raylan Givens from 'Justified' would be proud. My little one has sprouted wings and learned to fly."

"Darcy Gaughan, golden eagle. Look out, baby." She scratched her ear. "Liam's going to be here, too. In case our murderer makes a run for it, and we need to block the exit."

Char nodded. "What do we do if the murderer doesn't show?"

Darcy had anticipated the question. Her call with Sophia the previous evening confirmed her theory. If it was, in fact, correct, the murderer should be trying to get as far from Marysburg, Indiana, as possible.

The thing was, missing the jam session wouldn't go unnoticed. A well-timed comment from Darcy could lead to a lot of uncomfortable questions directed toward the entourage's absent member.

No. She was betting that the murderer was arrogant enough to think they could attend the show, then take off without a blemish to their reputation. The murderer didn't know Darcy Gaughan, though.

People familiar with Darcy knew it was a mistake to underestimate her. That was the critical mistake the murderer had made. And they were going to pay for it.

A bit later, Darcy was going through the proposed set list with the performers when three women entered the store. They were accompanied by Heather Ewing.

"What's she doing here?" Drew adjusted a tuning head on his bass guitar. "Figured she'd never want to see this town ever again."

"I invited her." Darcy went to greet the foursome. "Sophia, I'm so glad you could make it on such short notice."

"Thank you for inviting us. It was very kind of Ms. Ewing to pick us up at the airport." Derek's widow introduced her two daughters, Paris and Savannah, to Darcy. "We appreciate you going to all the trouble to put this on."

"It's been no trouble at all." Darcy took Sophia's hand in hers. "It's the least those of us here at Marysburg Music could do. As you can see, his band thought so, too."

Paris, the taller of the two daughters, who looked to be about Darcy's age, crossed her arms. "We've come a long way. Do you really know who killed our dad?"

Darcy glanced at Sophia. When the woman nodded, Darcy gestured toward the back of the store. "How about we have this conversation in private?"

Once they were behind closed doors, Darcy confirmed that yes, she knew who murdered Derek.

"Why haven't you called the police?" Savannah pushed a few strands of her brown hair behind an ear.

"Girls, we discussed this already." Sophia's cross tone caused Darcy to take a half-step backward. The woman had seemed so cool and collected at Selena's the other night. Then again, multiple gin and tonics could do that to a person.

"You all must be wiped out from your traveling. Are you hungry? Can I get you something to drink?" Darcy was a big believer in the notion of Hoosier Hospitality. The least she could do for these women was provide some refreshment.

"I just want to see the person who murdered my dad being taken away in the back seat of a squad car," Savannah said. "Dad might have been a P.O.S. Killing him wasn't right, though."

"Tell you what." Darcy picked up her cell phone. "I'm going to order a little spread for you from Selena's, the place your mom and I chatted last Saturday. If you want to chill back here, make yourselves at home. Of course, you're more than welcome to take a look around the store or go for a walk. Heather would be happy to show you around."

Paris jetted out the door for a walk without hesitation. Savannah, who was living in the New York City area, wanted to see what the small-town record store had to offer.

"I think I'll stay back here. It's hard to see the faces of the band and crew, knowing one of them murdered Derek." Sophia took the seat behind the desk when Darcy offered it to her. "You know, I can't escape the irony. There were so many times I got so angry that I thought or said I wanted him dead. And now that he's gone, I miss him. And I never got a chance to say goodbye."

Darcy's heart broke for the woman. Their phone call the previous night had left her jaw on the floor on more than one occasion. Among the other bombshells was the fact that the man Rafe had seen Sophia having drinks with was an old friend who'd recently been diagnosed with cancer. She'd kept that reason for the visit to herself since Derek had a history of unreasonable jealousy of her male friends.

The biggest revelation was that the stories claiming Derek was harassing women again were just that.

Stories. Nothing more.

Evidently, Brian had thought it would be a good idea to drop hints that Derek Tufnell, one of the pre-eminent bad boys of rock history, was on the road and ready to have a good time. The rumors would increase journalistic interest in the tour. That, in turn, would lead to increased publicity and corresponding ticket sales. Evidently, Brian McGuinness was a big believer in the cliché that there's no such thing as bad publicity.

To top the conversation off, Darcy learned that she had misinterpreted her initial conversation with Gwen. She wanted to rectify that right now.

"Do you mind if I ask Gwen to join us? She has some helpful information. She just doesn't realize it."

With Sophia's assent, Darcy brought her fellow drummer into the office.

"Gwen, I owe you an apology. When you and I first talked, I totally misunderstood what you were trying to tell me. I wanted to clear things up, and I think Sophia can help." Darcy held out her phone. There was a photo on the screen. "Do you recognize this man?"

"As a matter of fact, I do."

"To borrow a tennis term, Sophia." Darcy smiled. "I believe we have game, set, and match."

A few hours later, Darcy rose from her drum kit to a generous round of applause. Peter and Izzy exchanged wide grins with her. They'd just finished a jazzy interpretation of the classic soul tune "Am I the Same Girl?"

by Barbara Acklin. Izzy had nailed absolutely nailed the horn section while Peter had masterfully merged the keyboards and bass parts into a single, infectious bass groove that had the packed audience clapping along.

"I hope my extremely average singing wasn't too distracting." The assemblage laughed at Darcy's quip. "These young people can play. Peter, Izzy, take another bow."

Marysburg Music was packed, just as she'd hoped. Those in attendance were also in a good mood, which was even more important. It would make catching the murderer that much easier. A happy crowd would make for a cooperative crowd. At least, that was the hope. There was more music to play, though. After all, they were together to remember a man who, as it turned out, had stayed true to his promises.

Darcy chatted up the gathering while Gwen and Drew joined her and Peter onstage. "We've got a little surprise for you all before we ask Hambone to join us up here. When I asked Gwen if she'd join us for this little jam session, she said she'd do it on one condition. You want to tell them what that was?"

"Oh yeah." Gwen kicked off a few bass beats for emphasis. "I am here, on this stage, with the woman who founded Pixie Dust, one of my favorite bands, to play some of their songs."

She counted to three on her drumsticks, and the foursome tore into the Dust crowd favorite "Bite Me." Darcy had been worried she might ending up having to strain her vocal cords to match the fierce singing the song required. It turned out not to be a problem. In fact, it felt exhilarating.

Her position in front of the stage allowed her to keep an eye on the crowd, too.

It was gratifying to see how many people were recording the performance on their phones. Yeah, that free publicity thing couldn't be beat. When the song ended, the crowd burst into fervent applause that rattled the wall hangings.

"Thanks everyone." Darcy grinned. "Hold on tight because you ain't seen nothing yet. In a bit, we've got something you're never going to forget."

The foursome of Darcy, Peter, Drew, and Gwen played another Dust tune, "(Don't Hate Me) Sedate Me," to even more clapping and foot stomping.

When Liam shouted out a request for one more, Darcy shook her head.

"That's all my throat can handle. Besides, we're here to honor Derek Tufnell, rock and blues legend, am I right? So, let's get his friend and long-time collaborator up here on stage and play some Derek music. Let's hear it for Hambone Barclay, everyone."

As Hambone got situated, Darcy nodded to Charlotte. The woman went into the store's office, returning a moment later with Cameron Jessup.

All the pieces were in position on the chessboard. It was time for the headline performance to begin.

Chapter Twenty-Six

The group performed a laidback, mid-tempo version of "Keep on Knockin'." Darcy did her best to emulate Derek's legendary gravel-infused vocals. With the band in fine form, the bluesy boogie tune had everyone in the store grooving to the funky beat Gwen laid down.

As the song progressed, she made a point to make sure each musician performed a solo. After all, it was the last time the quartet behind her would play together for a long, long time. If ever.

When the song ended, Darcy hugged Peter and exchanged high-fives with Gwen and Drew. She pointed her finger at Hambone.

"How about another round of applause for that guy behind the keyboards." She clapped along with the crowd. "You and Derek wrote that song together, didn't you?"

"We did." He tipped his cowboy hat to the cheering audience. "Many moons ago."

"That's so cool." Darcy turned her gaze from Hambone to the crowd. "Something you all might not know is that back in the day, Derek and Hambone had an arrangement that when they wrote songs together, Derek was listed as the songwriter even when it was a collaborative effort. Pretty darn humble on Hambone's part to let Derek take all the credit."

She shot a quick look at Jessup. He was leaning against the sales counter with his hands in his pockets. His lips were curled up at one end. To his credit, he was keeping his mouth shut while Darcy continued to set the scene.

"He was my best friend." Hambone played a few notes on his keyboard. "That's what friends do."

"Which is weird because you didn't credit the actual songwriter on "Keep on Knockin."

"Say what?" Hambone took a drink from a water bottle as a low murmur rippled through the crowd.

"My apologies for bringing up some bad memories, folks, but this is important to Derek's legacy. A legacy someone in this room tried to destroy."

The crowd's murmuring grew to a full-throated din. Darcy didn't do anything to calm it. She wanted the murderer to feel the indignation. The anger.

She wanted the murderer to sweat.

"Derek's murder touched us all. Hurt us all. Well." She shrugged. "Well, most of us."

"Darcy, I don't think this is the time—"

"This is totally the time, Brian." She gave Derek's producer her most anger-filled stare. He'd been inching toward the stage. No doubt, it was an effort to get her to shut up.

She wasn't going to let him do it.

"When I started asking questions about his murder, it didn't take long to see a lot of people wanted Derek dead. That makes me so angry because he really had changed. Despite the awful rumors Brian started."

Now it was the producer's turn to take a step back. He caught himself and narrowed his gaze at her. "Enough's enough. Darcy. Whatever prank you're trying to pull, it isn't funny."

"Hey." A woman's voice carried over the din. It was Charlotte. "Let her speak."

The tension in the room was rising like the thermometer by Darcy's back door on a sunny July day.

"You may have heard some nasty rumors going around that Derek was drinking and harassing women again." A majority of the crowd nodded. "What you may not know is that they were stories. Totally made up. Nothing more, nothing less. And Brian McGuinness, Derek's producer, started them. Isn't that right, Gwen?"

"It is." The drummer got to her feet, taking a mic in her hand. "The worst thing Derek ever did to me was getting a little over-friendly. He never pressured me into anything. In fact, I was the one pressuring him. He'd been keeping a secret for a long time. I was trying to get him to come clean about it."

"What secret?" The question was shouted by Hank, who had stationed himself near the exit. His phone was in his hand. He was ready to call the police if needed.

"Don't worry. We'll get there," Darcy said. "Let's not short-circuit our trip down memory lane. Derek deserves to have the whole truth come out. Isn't that right, Sophia?"

Derek's widow spread her hands out wide. "My daughters and I came all this way. We want the whole show. You were saying?"

"That Brian's story doesn't end there." She paused for effect. "On the night Derek died, two witnesses saw Brian tell a woman that Derek was worth more dead than alive. Makes you wonder how serious he was about that, especially since he was the one that delivered the poisoned water to the theater."

As all gazes moved to Brian, he backed up against the wall. Darcy stifled a laugh as, for once, she was seeing the literal definition of being backed against the wall in action.

"I told you." He pointed at Darcy. "Hambone gave me the water. All I did was take it inside."

"I'm sorry, Sophia." He turned to look the woman in the eye. "Yes, I said it. But I was wrong. Derek was in top form."

"Are you still planning on releasing the recording of the concert?" Sophia moved toward him. "You'll make a lot of money doing that, won't you?"

"Well, I…" He waved his hands in circles as if he was hoping they would generate a reasonable response and send it to his brain.

"That's okay, Sophia. He's not the only one I want to send a shout-out to this evening." Darcy sat on a stool Peter handed to her. "Because it's true. He didn't deliver the poisoned water to Derek's dressing room. The lovely and talented tour manager extraordinaire Vanessa Perez took care of that."

"No. Don't you dare drag me into this." Vanessa made a beeline for Darcy.

Paris and Savannah cut her off.

"And yet you've already signed with another band for a European tour. Bigger venues. Higher profile. More money. Or do I have all those things wrong?"

She stopped struggling as her mouth morphed into a large O. With wide eyes, she looked to her left, then to her right. Nobody was coming to her aid.

"Fine, all of that is true. With Derek gone, I needed a new gig."

"Ah, yes." Darcy wagged her finger at Vanessa. "A new gig. Even though you made a big deal of talking about your plans to take Derek's tour to bigger and better heights. After this tour was over, of course. And now that it is, you didn't want to lose out on a working trip to Europe, eh?"

"No. You're taking things out of context. Why are you doing this to us?"

"I'll tell you." Darcy stepped off the stage and got right up into Vanessa's face. "Because Derek's family deserves to know the truth. He was in your way. Just like he was in Brian's way.

"The two of you lied about him and took advantage of him. For a while, I thought you even conspired to murder him." She stepped back up on the stage. "But you didn't. Someone else took advantage of you both to do that."

"It was Drew." Hambone pointed a finger at the guitarist. "He told me he overheard Derek and Gwen fighting on the last day of rehearsal. How could he do such a horrible thing?"

"He didn't." Darcy put her arm around Drew. "Want to tell everyone what you and Derek were arguing about, Gwen?"

The young drummer came to the front of the stage. "When I was hired, I didn't know much of Derek's catalog. When I started learning his songs, I discovered something. I'd heard "Keep on Knockin,'" or something almost exactly the same, before. I asked my parents about it."

"What did they tell you," Sophia asked.

"That before I was born, there was a band that played bars, festivals, and things like that in the Ann Arbor, Michigan area. They never made it big, but they had a song that sounded just like "Keep on Knockin'. That was the song Cameron Jessup sued Derek over. Derek didn't steal it from Cameron, though." Gwen pointed a finger to her right. "Hambone Barclay did."

The room erupted in a cacophony of shouts and screams as accusations were flung and fans tried to get to Hambone.

Liam waded through the crowd to join Peter, forcing people back from the stage. For all intents and purposes, Hambone was trapped there.

"That's what I was arguing with Derek about," Gwen said. "I was telling him he needed to make things right by Mr. Jessup. When we were on the tour bus the day of the show, he told me he was going to be making an announcement in a few days."

The woman leaned against Darcy. Her admission had taken the wind out of her sails.

"That's why Derek sent you that letter, Cameron." Darcy looked him in the eye. "You were right all along. The thing is, Derek didn't know the song was stolen. Hambone got ahold of it and told Derek he wrote it."

"That's not true." Hambone wiped a bead of sweat from his brow.

Darcy turned on him. "It's also why you were so anxious to sell the portion of Derek's music catalog you own. I overheard your conversation the other day. So, what happened? Did Derek confront you and tell you it was time to pay the piper?"

"It wasn't like that." He looked around and edged his way to the back of the stage, like he was going to make a break for it out the store's emergency exit in the back.

"Your stake in his catalog is worth millions. You told me the other day you weren't happy with how lean the tour staff was. You were unhappy and facing the loss of a chunk of change when Derek finally confessed and revealed you were the one who stole the song. That's why he had to die, wasn't it?"

Hambone forced out a laugh. It ended when Peter cut off his escape route.

"Even if this whole fantasy you've woven is true, you can't prove a thing."

"Sure, I can." She stepped within a few feet of him. "When Derek told you his plans to admit you stole the song, you decided to take his life instead of face the consequences of your actions. You took advantage of Brian's lies about Derek drinking again and figured out what poison made someone look intoxicated."

As if on cue, Paul Gerard began working his way through the crowd. He had a brown paper bag in his hand.

"Time was short, so you had to work with what you could get your hands on. Derek's fancy water had arrived. Thanks to the flavoring, he'd never be able to tell the difference between safe bottles and poisoned ones. As for the antifreeze, the bus always kept an extra jug on hand in case of a breakdown in the middle of nowhere. Isn't that right, Vanessa?"

The woman was silent for a moment, apparently deciding whether it was a good idea for her to say anything. Then she nodded.

"Yes. That's right. It would have been stored below, with the rest of the cargo."

"Which meant nobody would notice when you rolled out from rehearsals in Boston that it was missing. Or a six-pack of the water, either." Darcy faced Barclay. "Hambone, you told me that you don't sleep well at night. Which made it easy for you to poison the bottles when everyone else was asleep. All you had to do was make sure your cabin curtain was drawn, sit up, pour some water from each bottle into a cup, replace the water with the corresponding amount of antifreeze, and your work was done."

A sob came from the crowd. It was Savannah. When Darcy looked at her, she raised her chin, as if to tell Darcy to keep going.

"Then, when you all arrived here in town, you slipped the poisoned bottles into the cargo bay during all the unloading activity."

"You're a good storyteller. Maybe you should write mystery books instead of running a record store." Hambone cracked his knuckles. "If I actually did what you say, where's the bottle of antifreeze I supposedly stole?"

"Right here." Paul pulled it out of the bag and held it high for all to see. "We found it behind a building a block away from the theater. The serial number on the bottle matches up with a batch that was sold at an automotive supply store in the Boston area."

"Boston, huh." Darcy turned her attention from Paul to Hambone. "Isn't that where you all had rehearsals?"

Hambone stood still for a moment as a hush fell over the crowd. Then he rammed his elbow into Peter's chest. The young man went down in a heap

192

as the older one made a move for the exit in the back.

He'd leapt from the stage by the time people started shouting to stop him. Before anyone else could get to him, though, a copper disc the size of a pizza zinged through the air and hit him in the back of the head.

The man fell in a heap.

"Got him." Gwen smiled, her cheeks turning a bright pink. She was standing next to Darcy's drumkit. The crash cymbal was missing. It was now lying on the floor, slightly bent, next to a prone Hambone.

Chapter Twenty-Seven

"I still can't believe you threw one of my cymbals at him." Darcy shook her head but raised her glass of lemonade to Gwen. "It was a good shot. Gotta give you that. Nice payback for him taking me out on the trail, too."

By the time Paul, with an assist from Liam, corralled a resisting Hambone into a Marysburg PD squad car, the memorial jam session had come to an unexpected, if not memorable, end. A little while later, two uniformed officers arrived. They'd taken contact information from everyone in the store before letting people leave.

Now, there were only a handful of folks left. They were hanging around the stage area. Darcy was sitting on a stool in between Hank and Charlotte. Peter was in the office, being interviewed by one of the uniformed officers. Liam sat behind the cash register, talking to the other one.

"To be honest, I always wanted to do that. It felt like I was a rock and roll Captain America." Gwen bumped her shoulder against Drew's. "I'm thankful this guy noticed what I was up to and ducked."

The guitarist ran his fingers through his hair. "I got a haircut right before we left Boston. I didn't feel like getting another one."

The group laughed. Even Derek's daughters joined their mother in a chuckle.

"Well, I can't thank you all enough for exposing my husband's murderer." Sophia dabbed a tissue at the corners of her eyes. "It's a relief that now everyone knows the stories about the drinking and harassment were only stories."

"And, um." Paris went to Cameron and extended her hand. "I'm really sorry about my dad and Barclay plagiarizing your song. That was wrong. My mom, my sister, and I want to make things right."

"I appreciate that." He took her hand in his. "I'm still trying to get my head around the fact that your dad never knew where the song came from."

"You'd be surprised," Sophia said. "Derek and Barclay had worked together for a long time. They hadn't had a hit for a while, so when Hambone said he had a new idea for a song, Derek didn't question it."

Darcy let out a sad sigh. "Derek was the lead singer. People believed him during the trial. And Hambone was convincing enough that he got away it."

"What'll happen now?" Izzy plopped down on the seat behind the keyboard stand. She'd been busy tidying up while the rest of those sticking around decompressed.

The group was silent. After a time, one by one, heads turned in Darcy's direction.

She put her hands up. "Don't look at me. I just figured out who the murderer is. I leave it to people who are smarter than me to take it from there."

The front door opened. There had been so many people going in and out that there was no point in locking up just yet.

"I'm sorry. We're closed." Darcy got to her feet. "Oh, hi Paul. We're all waiting for our turn to be interviewed. Can I help you with anything?"

"No." The police officer joined them. "Just wanted to stop by to give you all some good news. Once we got Mr. Barclay to the station and read him his rights, he broke down and gave us a full confession. The Detective-Sergeant is getting his statement down as we speak."

Charlotte extended her fist toward Darcy for a knuckle bump. "And Darcy Gaughan does it again."

"I had a lot of help." Darcy's cheeks got warm. At times like this, she wondered if she'd ever become comfortable receiving a compliment. She wasn't there yet, so she changed the subject. "Gwen's not in any trouble, is she?"

"She was attempting to subdue a fleeing murder suspect." Paul shrugged.

"Ms. Crane, your method of accomplishing that was unorthodox, to say the least, but under the circumstances, I don't think you have anything to worry about."

"He's not injured, then," Gwen asked. Before Paul could respond, she hurried on. "Hey, I just want to make sure that guy has to face the music in a court of law."

"Face the music. That's a good one, yesi." Peter tapped Izzy on the shoulder. "You're next in the interrogation room."

"It's not an interrogation," Darcy said when Izzy looked at her with fear in her eyes. "The officer wants to know what you saw and heard. Nothing more, nothing less. Right, Paul?"

"That's correct, Miss Izzy." He held out his hand. "If you want, I'll sit with you during the interview."

Izzy blinked, then the corners of her lips curved up in a dreamy smile. "Sure."

"She going to be okay back there with two cops all by herself?" Peter frowned. A difficult experience with a cop from a neighboring town, all due to the color of Peter's skin, had left him distrustful of the police.

"Paul's got her back." Darcy gave Peter a reassuring hug. "Just like I've got yours."

"Good to see you have things under control, Darc." Jenna stood in the entryway. She was holding two large plastic bags. "I heard there was some unexpected excitement here tonight. Who wants something to snack on while you tell me what I missed?"

Peter and Drew practically raced across the store to find out what goodies Jenna had provided.

While they rummaged through the sacks, Paris cleared her throat. "What happens now?"

Savannah wandered over to the pastries Jenna had set out on the sales counter. "Now that we know who killed my dad, I'd like to get back home as soon as possible."

"Once we get everyone's statements, you're all free to go." Paul handed a business card to Sophia. "If you have any questions, please don't hesitate to reach out."

The group stayed together as the interviews proceeded. It was like they'd formed a tight-knit bond nobody wanted to break. Sophia was the last of Derek's family to give a statement. When she was finished, she shook Paul's hand. "Thank you. And thanks to all of you who helped catch Derek's killer. Mr. Jessup, we'll be in touch."

"I never wanted things to end this way. I've always been a fan of your husband's music." Cameron's voice became unsteady. "I'm truly sorry for you and your daughters' loss."

To Darcy's utter astonishment. Sophia hugged him. They exchanged a few words, then she put one arm around Savannah, the other around Paris. With Heather by their side to provide emotional support, they left the building.

Eventually, the officers completed the interviews. Only Darcy, her Marysburg Music team, Drew, and Gwen remained. When Paul and the uniformed officers left, Hank looked at his boss.

"While we were waiting to be interviewed, I counted out the register." He chuckled. "Despite how things ended, it was a good day for the store. I can take it to the bank if you want."

"I'll take care of it." Darcy put her hands on her hips and leaned forward to stretch her back. "It's been a crazy day. You all were wonderful. I don't have the words for how much it means to me that every person in this room was so willing to stick their necks out to catch a murderer. Go home, everyone. Hug someone who matters to you. Tomorrow's a new day full of new possibilities."

Drew was the first to leave. He made his goodbyes brief as he was looking forward to starting the drive home to his family as soon as possible.

Hank and Char walked out together. The older man had insisted on escorting her to her car. Despite her objections, which were halfhearted at most, he wouldn't take no for an answer. Given the unprecedented events of the evening, their desire to stick together, even for a little while longer, was totally understandable.

Liam took Darcy in his arms. "I'm so proud of you. I can drive you home if you want. You must be wiped out."

She squeezed him tight, then kissed him on the cheek. He was a great almost-boyfriend. The kind of man Darcy wanted in her life. Was there more to the relationship? Maybe. She wasn't interested in thinking about that at the moment.

"You've had a long day too. I'll check in with you tomorrow. Let you know how my debrief with the Detective-Sergeant goes." Paul had taken her witness statement. When they were finished, he told her that Kaitlin had follow-up questions and expected to see her at the police station at nine sharp.

When she agreed, she followed Liam to the door and, after exchanging a goodnight kiss, locked it. Much to her surprise, she found she still wasn't alone. Gwen, Peter, and Izzy were deep in conversation. Darcy didn't want to interrupt, but it was almost eleven. Ringo was waiting at home and was not going to be happy with her for delaying his dinner.

"Closing time, people. I don't know who said it first, but it's true. You don't have to go home, but you can't stay here."

"Sorry, Boss." Peter got to his feet. "We were talking music. Gwen was giving us some pointers."

"These two are really talented. I was just telling them to keep at it." Gwen handed her phone to Izzy. "Put your digits in there. I want to know how things go for you both."

"About that, Boss." Peter flashed his million-dollar smile. "We were wondering. Since the jam session didn't finish, would it be okay if we play at open mic night Saturday?"

"Fine by me." Darcy sat down next to Izzy. "My elbow's a little sore from tonight, so I don't think I'll be able to sit in with you. Are you comfortable with performing as a duo?"

"Oh, we're not going to do that. We kind of have a replacement drummer already." Izzy's cheeks pinked up.

"Cool. Is it one of your classmates?"

"Actually, it's me," Gwen said. "I love these two and don't have to be anywhere at the moment. I haven't played jazz in a while, so I thought it might be fun. I hope you don't mind."

"Mind?" Darcy laughed. It was a long, tension-releasing laugh that she'd been needing. It felt *so* good. "Heck no, I don't mind. You gotta promise me one thing, though."

"What's that," Izzy and Peter asked in unison.

Darcy shot a look at Gwen. "You have to work one Pixie Dust song into your set."

This time it was Gwen's turn to laugh. "I think that can be arranged."

Chapter Twenty-Eight

Darcy pulled open the door to the police station ten minutes after nine. Her late arrival was no accident or oversight. While she would admit to friends that her tardiness was a childish move, she didn't care. Kaitlin Rosengarten had bullied and belittled Darcy long enough.

No more.

"Detective-Sergeant, how are you?" She placed a muffin from Jenna's on the cop's desk. It was even a fresh one, not something left over from the previous night.

"I'm a busy woman, and you're late. I don't appreciate having my time wasted." Kaitlin stabbed at her keyboard with the ferocity of an angry bear.

"Seems to me since Derek Tufnell's murder has been solved, you'd have some time on your hands. Maybe even enough to say thank you. Again."

"Whatever." The woman rolled her eyes, then pointed a finger at Darcy. "You should know this department doesn't need you playing detective. Our investigation was on good footing. We would have made an arrest soon."

Darcy put up her hands as if in surrender. "I don't doubt that. Maybe in the future, you'll be able to make sure there are no leaks about suspects. That way, I won't have to get involved to clear my name."

Kaitlin opened her mouth, then shut it. Point for Darcy. Not that she was counting, of course. But she was.

"I've gone over your statement Officer Gerard took last night. Why didn't you come to me with the information you had? I mean, that is our job, after all."

"I thought about it. Then I remembered your history of taking anything I say with a grain of salt. I didn't want to risk giving Barclay a chance to get out of town while you debated the trustworthiness of my info."

"And yet Officer Gerard was there. With a key piece of evidence." Kaitlin stared at Darcy. "Any idea why he happened to be there?"

Darcy didn't have the energy or inclination to play games. She'd been up way too late apologizing to Ringo. Besides, she'd solved two murders in her town. She didn't feel the need to explain herself to the Detective-Sergeant or anyone else.

"I suppose he wanted to be there for the jam session. He's a smart guy. Probably figured with so many suspects there, it was a good idea to be prepared." Darcy shrugged. "Seems to me that's a question you should ask him."

"I'll leave that to the chief." Kaitlin blew out a breath and leaned back in her chair. "So you can start planning your own little celebration. I have news for you. I'm leaving the department. Taking a detective position with the Fort Wayne PD. Try not to shed too many tears over my departure."

Darcy sat in stunned silence for a while. People around town had told her that Kaitlin had her eye on a gig in a bigger town. Darcy hadn't paid any attention to that rumor, though. Believing gossip was a dangerous thing to do.

She wouldn't celebrate the woman's upcoming departure, though. If there was one thing Darcy had learned recently, it was people should do what they can to be happy. If moving from small-town Marysburg, with its ten thousand residents, to the second largest city in Indiana, with over three hundred thousand residents, was going to make Kaitlin happy, good for her.

Darcy extended her hand. "Best of luck to you, Detective-Sergeant. The people of Fort Fun are in good hands with you looking out for them."

They shook, then Kaitlin flicked her fingers at Darcy to dismiss her. "Thanks. Now, get out of here before I decide to throw you in the lock-up one more time, for old times' sake."

Darcy didn't need to be told twice.

The next few days went by at a leisurely pace compared to the previous ten days. With no murder case taking up her time and stressing her out, Darcy took things easy. Though she did begin to prepare for Small Business Saturday, which was now only a month away. There was always something on the horizon, after all.

On Saturday afternoon, she was behind the cash register, ringing up a sale when Peter arrived with his bass in its carrying case. Izzy and Gwen were right behind him.

"Ready for some hot jazz tonight, Boss?"

"I am." Darcy exchanged a high-five with him as he strolled to the stage. "Do I get an inside scoop on the setlist?"

"Sorry. That would spoil the surprise." Izzy placed her tenor saxophone on a stand near the front of the stage. Next to it, she placed a larger baritone sax.

Darcy looked at Gwen. "Come on, show this has-been a little drummer love."

The woman shook her head. "It's their gig. I've been sworn to secrecy."

"Well, whatever y'all are going to play, I'm looking forward to it. I'm sure it's going to be amazing."

And amazing the forty-five-minute set was. Each song the trio performed for the crowd, which was much larger than Darcy had anticipated, was familiar, but had a unique take to it. Even when they performed the Pixie Dust tune "Bottom's Up," the threesome breathed new life into the song. Their performance took an angry punk song and transformed it into a funky tune that had the younger people in the audience literally dancing in the aisles.

When the show ended, Gwen, Izzy, and Peter spent a full thirty minutes chatting with fans, friends, and other musicians who had performed, taking selfies with them, and signing autographs.

"With young people like that performing, the future of music's bright, don't you think?" Charlotte handed Darcy a tissue.

She dabbed at her eyes with it. Her emotional response to the performance had caught her by surprise. It made her feel like she was floating on air, though. She was going to need a few more tissues, though.

"Yeah." She hugged Char. "I can't wait to see what the future has in store. For them and for us."

Always finding something to look forward to. For Darcy Gaughan, that was turning out to be a great approach to life.

Acknowledgements

I'd like to thank my wonderful editor Shawn Reilly Simmons and the entire team at Level Best Books for their support of the Darcy Gaughan Mysteries. Thanks also go to my agent, Dawn Dowdle, for her belief in a former punk rocker turned record store owner.

About the Author

J.C. Kenney is the bestselling author of The Allie Cobb Mysteries, The Darcy Gaughan Mysteries, and The Elmo Simpson Mysteries. He's also the co-host of The Bookish Hour webcast. His debut, A Literal Mess, was a finalist for a Muse Medallion from the Cat Writers' Association in mystery fiction. When he's not writing, you can find him following IndyCar racing or listening to music. He has two grown children and lives in Indianapolis with his wife and a cat. You can find him at www.jckenney.com.

SOCIAL MEDIA HANDLES:
  https://www.jckenney.com
  https://www.facebook.com/JCKenney1
  https://www.instagram.com/j.c.kenney
  https://goodreads.com/jckenney

AUTHOR WEBSITE:
  www.jckenney.com

Also by J.C. Kenney

The Darcy Gaughan Mysteries
  Record Store Reckoning

The Allie Cobb Mysteries
  A Literal Mess
  A Genuine Fix
  A Mysterious Mix Up
  A Deadly Discovery
  The Dead of Winter
  A Parting Shot

www.ingramcontent.com/pod-product-compliance
Lightning Source LLC
Chambersburg PA
CBHW030425120726
47903CB00003B/822